JOSEPH BRUCHAC

peacemaker

DIAL BOOKS FOR YOUNG READERS

DIAL BOOKS FOR YOUNG READERS
An imprint of Penguin Random House LLC, New York

First published in the United States of America by Dial Books for Young Readers,
an imprint of Penguin Random House LLC, 2021

Copyright © 2021 by Joseph Bruchac
Map © 2021 by Cerise Steel

Visit us online at penguinrandomhouse.com.

Library of Congress Cataloging-in-Publication Data is available.

Printed in the United States of America

ISBN 9781984815378

10 9 8 7 6 5 4 3 2 1

Design by Cerise Steel
Text set in Apollo MT Pro

To Ray Tehanetorens Fadden, Alice Dewasentah
Papineau, Tom Sakokwenionkwas Porter,
Audrey Gonwaiani Shenandoah, and Chief Jake
Tekaronianeken Swamp — Friends, Teachers, and true
Wisdom Keepers to whom I will always be grateful.

chapter one
THE HUNTERS

"Where did the boy go?" an angry voice asked.

"He can't be far. Grab him as soon as you see him!" The voice that answered was calm but cold.

They were, indeed, close to Okwaho's hiding place in the blackberry tangles. It was not yet the time of the fall rains, when it would be safe to burn away the dried undergrowth. So the half-green bushes on his side of the trail were still thick. Even now, with the midday light of Elder Brother Sun shining brightly down on the land, it was dark within the bushes where he hid.

He began to sing—not out loud, but inside his mind. Songs have power. His uncle, At the Edge of the Sky, had taught him that, praised him for his singing.

You will not see me.
You will not see me.
You will pass on by.
You will pass on by.

They were getting even closer. Though they were not speaking now, he could hear not only their feet crushing the twigs on the path but also their heavy breathing.

If I hadn't crawled in here, he thought, *I'd be caught now. A captive like Tawis.* The thought of what had just happened to his friend troubled him more than what might happen to him.

The two of them had gone together to the stream that flowed into the small river near their village. They knew that fishing there would be better, that at this time of the year big trout sometimes left the main water to run upstream into the creeks. It had not been that far for them to walk, no longer than the time for Elder Brother Sun to rise another hand's width up into the sky. And despite the fact that there was always the threat of enemies, things had been calm for their little community since the decision to leave the big village of Onondaga.

There were only fourteen families, fifty people altogether, who made that decision. It had been suggested first by the women who were the heads of those families and the men had agreed. All of them had lost friends and family members to the conflict that never ended. As long as they remained in the big village, led by Atatarho, their giant chief whose every thought was of war, more of those they loved would die.

Burnt Hair and Okwaho's father, Holds the Door Open, had been chosen to announce their decision to the great chief. Atatarho had stared at them with anger in his eyes. For a few breaths it seemed as if he would either forbid them to leave or have them punished. Then the giant war chief had shaken his head, the black snakes tied into his hair writhing as he did so.

"You are no help to me if you will not fight," Atatarho growled. "Go. See what your foolish decision brings you. But your dogs cannot go with you. They stay here. They will help guard our village from enemies, and take the place of you weaklings."

As the group left the village, no one had spoken to wish them a good journey and good health. Instead, everyone who was not coming with them looked away. All except one person: Clouds Forming, who was the best friend of Okwaho and Tawis. She stood defiantly at the gate, watching them depart. Though she did not speak aloud, Okwaho saw the words she was forming with her mouth.

Be strong, my brothers. We will meet again.

When the fourteen families decided to leave the big village, the family of Clouds Forming had not agreed to go with them. They were of the same clan and family as Atatarho, the powerful warrior chief. There was no way anyone in his family could go against their kinsman's word. Even if they had not feared his anger, their first loyalty was to their powerful relative.

It had been five moons since their departure from the big village. The hard times of constant fighting that cost the lives of so many had seemed far behind them to the two boys. It was the sort of warm day that sometimes comes after the leaves have begun to change color. The stream where they knew there were big trout was not that far from their hidden village. Surely no danger could come to them there.

Even so, Okwaho and Tawis had been careful. They'd waited, looking around and listening before leaving the shelter of the forest and walking out onto the meadow that had been left when an old beaver dam had finally collapsed. The narrow but deep stream that wound its way through that meadow had spots eroded out under its banks by the current where good-sized fish might be found.

The two of them had walked along either side of the stream, staying low, moving slowly and keeping their eyes on the water. They knew that fish could feel the vibration of heavy feet and hide before being seen. Still, every time they caught sight of a trout facing into the current, tail moving lazily, that fish would quickly see them and dart for safety under a stone or under the stream bank.

Most of those fish were small, no bigger than the width of two hands, so they kept going. Then, just past the place where the spring-fed stream widened, they both saw it. A brook trout near the surface. Facing upstream, watching for any food the stream might bring its way, it was almost as long as one of Okwaho's arms. Big enough to provide a meal for both their families.

Sensing their presence, the trout dove, its square tail sending up a plume of spray.

"THERE!" Tawis had shouted. Then, realizing he needed to be quieter, he lowered his voice. "Under the stream bank on your side," he said, pointing with his lips toward the other place where a big old birch tree grew, its feathery roots caressed by the current. "Go for him. I'll keep watch."

Okwaho nodded and slid carefully into the water. For the type of fishing they were doing, being slow and quiet was important. He put his feet down on the stream bottom, finding his balance. The cool water was up to his waist. A song came into his mind, one for the big fish. It was a song that would calm it, ask it to give itself to them, thank its spirit for the sacrifice of its flesh.

Singing that new song softly, Okwaho began to move

forward, first one foot and then the other, like a stalking heron.

Okwaho looked up at Tawis on the other side, the stream wider here than an agile man could clear with a running jump.

Tawis nodded. "There," he said. "You are in the right place."

"Keep watch," Okwaho said. He began taking deep breaths. One, two, three, four. When his lungs were full, he leaned forward, bending his knees until his head was underwater.

He could see the dark hole circled by a tangle of tree roots. It was deeper than he'd thought. He'd have to pull his whole body inside to reach the huge trout.

Okwaho had not worried about how long that would take. He was very good at holding his breath for a long time. Also, as he moved forward, he could see a shaft of light from overhead at the back of the hole. It was open there to the air between the thick roots on the back of the large bankside birch. If he ran out of breath, all he had to do was stand up to get his head and shoulders out of the water. That shaft of light reflected off the tail of the big trout. The rest of its body was hidden where it had nosed into a crevice at the back of the hole.

My friend, Okwaho thought, sending his thought to the fish, *Swift Swimmer, I ask that you let me catch you. My family needs your help to provide food for us.*

Hooking one leg under a nearby root to keep himself from floating upward, he reached both hands forward slowly. He began to move his fingers as he touched the big fish, caressing its slippery side as he worked his way up toward its gills. Feeling the quiver of its life between his hands, he grasped it firmly, pulling it out of its hiding place. It didn't struggle, as if it was showing its agreement to be their food, knowing that they would respect it. That when it was taken from the water and the quiver of life left it, Tawis and he would speak those ancient words: May your spirit continue to swim.

Thank you for giving yourself to me, Okwaho thought as he turned inside the hole, holding the big trout to his chest, his fingers inside its gill slits. He made ready to thrust himself out and up to the surface.

But then he'd heard a sound. Even underwater, the sound reached him. It was a shout.

"NO!"

And at that same moment he felt the thudding vibrations of heavy feet.

He let go of the trout. He'd almost run out of breath, but he didn't dare leave the hole under the bank. That shout from Tawis had been meant as a warning. He pushed backward toward the place where the hole opened up between the tree roots. Then he stood up slowly so that his head broke the surface without making a sound.

He shook his head to clear the water from his ears. All that he could see to either side were the roots of the birch tree. It meant that he could not be seen. But he could hear. And what he heard made his heart pound.

"Where is your friend?" a harsh angry voice said.

"I was alone," answered a voice Okwaho recognized immediately as that of Tawis. "I was looking for fish by myself."

"Hah," another voice answered, a voice that sounded as cold as a winter wind. Like the first one who spoke, his accent was not that of an Onondaga. It sounded like that of one of the Standing Stone Nation, the Oneidas. "Do not lie to us. We saw two of you."

"No," Tawis said, his voice stubborn. "I was alone."

That word was followed by a sharp slapping sound. Though he could not see what had just happened with his eyes, Okwaho saw it all too clearly in his mind. His loyal friend was being hit for his defiance.

If only Clouds Forming had been with us, Okwaho thought. *She would have kept watch while we fished. With her keen eyes and ears she would have sensed trouble.*

Then another voice spoke, one that was calmer than the first two.

"Do not strike the boy again. He did not cry out when you hit him. I like that. I like his courage. Maybe my mother will adopt him."

"I have a mother already," Tawis replied.

The third man laughed. "Listen to him. Brave."

Okwaho reached up to grasp the roots above him. There looked to be enough space for him to pull himself up. He put one foot on a root that extended underwater, then lifted himself a finger's width at a time. Before long, his head and shoulders were above water. Still without making a sound, he pushed and pulled himself farther up until his whole upper body was out. The wide tree trunk still blocked his view. He leaned carefully to one side to look around the old tree. Now he could see the opposite bank.

There stood the three men, at the edge of the stream. One of them, perhaps the one with the calm voice, was holding Tawis by one arm. He was a tall, good-looking man, with blue curving lines, each ending in a star, tattooed across his cheeks. There was a smile on his face. In another circumstance, he appeared to be someone who would be pleasant to meet. That was not true of the other two men. One of them, the broad-shouldered one with big muscles, wore a scowl on his face. The second man was the tallest of the three. His head was shaved and half of his face was painted black. His face was expressionless, his eyes shining like those of a snake.

"It will do you no good to stay silent," he said. "Even if your friend gets away now, we will get him later.

We've seen how small your little village is. When we decide to come back with a large war party, we will get him after we have killed your few warriors."

Hearing those words, Okwaho's heart sank. *I should go back to our little village and warn everyone. But how can I leave Tawis?*

Not sure what he should do, Okwaho pulled himself up a little farther, starting to swing up and free his legs. But as he did so, one of the roots he was holding broke with a sharp snap. Okwaho froze.

Three pairs of eyes turned quickly in his direction. But not the eyes of Tawis.

"RUN!" Tawis shouted as he yanked his arm so quickly that he freed himself from the grasp of Calm Voice. Then he threw himself at the legs of the other two, sending them backward into the stream.

Okwaho had no weapon. He was only a boy and they were three grown men. And so, not so much because he wished to save himself, but more because he wanted to honor his friend's brave sacrifice, he knew he should do as Tawis said. He pushed himself up, scrambled to his feet.

"Hah-ah," Calm Voice laughed, grabbing Tawis by both arms. "You see what I mean. My mother will love this boy. You two catch his friend. Running will dry you out."

Okwaho had run as hard as he could, but his legs were not as long as those of the men pursuing him. Even though what Tawis had done gave him a head start, he knew from the sounds behind him they were gaining on him. So he had taken shelter in the bushes, hearing their voices come closer.

Okwaho clenched his fists. *If only I were a grown man. If only I had a weapon with me. Then I would make them sorry.*

Usually Okwaho was aggressive or ready to fight. He was not like Clouds Forming. A girl of the same age as him, she had been Okwaho's second-best friend. Gentle and strong, she was the perfect match for the both of them. She knew just what to say or do to calm Okwaho when he was angry, encourage Tawis when he was uncertain. She was also funny, always saying something to make them laugh. The three of them had always done things together before his family left the big village. Whenever they played such games as throwing spears or shooting arrows, it was Clouds Forming who was always best.

"Perhaps," she used to say to Okwaho, "when we are grown, I will be the one to go out and fight enemies while you will stay home and sing songs to our children."

Such teasing had never bothered him. Let her fight

if she wanted to fight. The one thing he could do much better than her was to make up songs. In fact, Clouds Forming admired him for that—despite her teasing. In one of her rare serious moments, she told him that.

"Being able to make up songs as you do, Okwaho," she said, placing her finger gently on his lips, "that is truly a gift from our Creator."

Okwaho always used to think that was what he wanted to do—make songs. He could still be a good hunter and one day a good father and uncle, but the thing he would do best of all would be the making of songs.

That was what he used to think. But now, now, his hands wanted nothing more than to hold a bow and loose one arrow after another at those enemies, those arrogant Standing Stone men.

It was no surprise that Standing Stone warriors had come into Onondaga lands to raid them. Less than a moon ago, Atatarho had led a hundred of his men on a raid against the nearest Standing Stone village, a long day's walk from Onondaga. Word of that raid sent out by Atatarho had reached their little community, even though none of their people took part in it. They heard how five Oneida boys and two women had been brought back—either to be adopted or treated as slaves. The Onondaga warriors who secretly visited relatives in their breakaway community had boasted of killing two Oneida men, as well.

But even though they'd heard word of that raid, no one in Okwaho's small village of only ten handfuls of people had expected they would be the target of any revenge attack. Everyone knew those fifty had left Onondaga to get away from fighting. They only wanted peace to grow their crops, hunt and fish, and take care of their families. Surely any raid would be against the big town of Onondaga, with its more than one thousand people. Not their tiny village. Also, they had thought it was well hidden—far back from any of the main trails.

We were wrong, Okwaho thought as he stayed crouched down in the thick tangle of the blackberry bushes. *Wrong. You cannot escape war.*

"See how the leaves on the trail are scuffed here?" Angry Voice growled. Even nearer to Okwaho than before. Too near.

"Ah," Cold Voice replied. "Yes. See that broken branch? And then the next? He went off the trail that way. We'll have him soon."

No. You won't. I broke those branches to lead you away from where I am now.

He kept his head down, his eyes closed, the words of the song—*you will pass on by*—repeating in his head.

An enemy may feel your gaze. That was what At the

Edge of the Sky taught him. For just a moment Okwaho felt again the pain of his uncle's death—at the hands of Standing Stone men like those now hunting him. It was like something smoldering inside him, that pain that he felt grow hotter every day, ready to burst into the flame of revenge.

It is not right that we seek to kill each other. Those had been his mother's words, even after her brother's body was brought back to their camp. *How could she still believe that?*

"Follow me," Cold Voice said. He sounded eager now. "He must be cutting across to the river trail."

"We'll catch him before he reaches the water," Angry Voice snarled.

Okwaho waited until the sounds of thudding feet could no longer be heard. Then he lifted his head slightly to peer up through a squinted eye. Neither of the men could be seen. But he did not rise up from where he lay. *Never assume that an enemy is not trying to deceive you by pretending to give up the chase and merely waiting for you to show yourself.*

He silently counted, slowly breathing in and out, until he reached ten. A chickadee came fluttering in and landed on a blackberry cane a hand's width from his face. It cocked its head to look at him.

"A-dee-dee-dee?" it said, as if to ask why he was still hiding. Then it began to pick at a dried berry.

"A-dee-dee-dee," Okwaho sang back to the bird, whose song was a message that the danger was past. "A-dee-dee-dee."

Chickadees were known to be friends of human beings, more so than any other bird. Okwaho knew the story of how, in the most ancient times, it was the chickadees who did something wonderful. It happened when the Good Mind, one of the twin boys who were the first to walk the earth in the shape of men, found himself in a contest with his grandmother, Sky Woman. She wrongly blamed the Good Mind for the death of his mother. She wanted to end all life on the earth and to then return to the sky. The Good Mind did not think that was right and convinced his grandmother to play the Bowl Game. Whichever of them did best would decide what would happen to all of Creation.

Back then, as now, that game was played using peach stones painted black on one side and white on the other. They would be placed in a wooden bowl. When that bowl was struck on the ground, the peach stones would be flipped up. The way they landed—with most either white side or black side up—would determine the winner.

When it was the Good Mind's turn, a flock of chickadees came and landed on his shoulder. *We will sacrifice our own heads to use as stones in the game,* they said. And they did just that. When the bowl was struck on the ground, their black and white heads flew up into the air singing and landed in just such a way that the Good Mind won.

It was said that losing the Bowl Game changed his grandmother's mind. Not only did she allow life to continue, when she returned to the sky, she became Grandmother Moon, looking down on the earth with a kind face.

Okwaho nodded at the chickadee. "Niaweh, little brother," he whispered. "Thank you for letting me know it is safe now to come out of my hiding place."

Still, despite the small black-capped bird's reassurance, Okwaho moved out slowly—a finger's width at a time—making almost no sound at all as he crawled from beneath the shelter of the thick tangle of blackberry canes. Staying on his belly, he pulled himself along a narrow tunnel that had been made by other creatures—rabbits probably—that used what had been his hiding place as their own safe haven. One sharp thorn scratched his cheek, but he paid no attention to it. A true warrior ignores pain.

A small red trickle of blood marked his face when he finally emerged. When he reached up a finger to touch it, he felt it leave a red line across his cheek—like one of the lines of red paint men put on their faces to show they are going to fight. He dropped his hand. He would leave that bloody line there.

According to the story his uncle had told him, those lines of red paint made on the faces of the warriors of all five of the nations—that had once lived together as brothers—came to be because of one man. Long ago, that young man fought a monster bear and defeated it—using only a stone knife. Before the young man's knife found the huge animal's heart, that bear's claws had raked across the man's face leaving lines of blood. Signs of courage, of determination to fight and win.

Okwaho came out of the tunnel through the blackberry vines. He looked either way, seeing no one. Still, he crouched for a moment on the trail, thinking about what he should do next. Should he follow the trail that led straight to their little village?

No.

The men who'd chased him might be turning back now. Not having seen him or found his trail, they might now be placing themselves to wait between where they had last seen him and his village downstream on Long Creek.

Once again, he wished that he were older, that he had a bow and arrows, a spear or a war club.

When you strike an enemy with a club, aim for the temple. That is where your enemy's skull will be the weakest.

That was what his uncle had told him, easily tossing his own war club with the round stone fastened in its head from one hand to the other as he spoke.

He pictured himself creeping up on them from behind—then striking!

But he was not a grown man.

It would take longer, but making a big circle would be the safest and wisest thing for Okwaho to do. He should head directly away from his home and then gradually turn to swing wide and approach it from the other direction. He might still reach home before Grandmother Moon's face rose into the sky.

Okwaho stood, took a deep breath, turned, and began to run.

chapter two
THE VILLAGE

Dusk was still two hands away from settling its blanket over the hills when Okwaho finally reached their small village nestled between the hills where Long Creek made a great bend. They called their hidden village Kanata. All the trees and brush had been cleared away for a circle around their village as far as any arrow might fly. It had taken much work, but now the land was open all the way down to the creek edge where the corn field had been planted.

Everyone thought they had chosen a good place to site this new village of theirs. Their crops would grow well at the edge of the creek, which flooded every year with the spring ice melt, leaving fertile silt behind when the waters receded. With the abundant deer, the many food and medicine plants in the forest, and their fall harvest of corn and beans and squash, life should have been good for them.

But with the constant threat of attack, the endless cycle of raid and counter-raid going on everywhere in their world, there was no time when they were not in an atmosphere of uncertainty. They were hidden, but they still might be found. And even though they sought peace, they still might have to fight to defend themselves. That was why they were still working on the palisade of upright logs planted in the earth around Kanata.

The lights of cooking fires gleamed through the chinks in those peeled upright pine logs that had been dug into the ground and then woven together with vines to make the strong stockade around their four longhouses.

As Okwaho made his way around Kanata's tall wall toward the single gateway that led inside, he saw a small group of people waiting there.

Two were men, both holding bows and arrows and guarding the entrance. One of those men was Burnt Hair, the uncle of Tawis. Seeing him made Okwaho's heart sink. Every boy's uncle was the most important man in his life. The bond between Burnt Hair and Tawis had always been a deep one, even more so after Tawis's much older brother, Tall Bird, had died while on a raid against the Swampy Land people. The other man was

Okwaho's father, Holds the Door Open. A tall woman who was turned away from them to look down the trail was between them. From the way she stood there, it was clear that she was anxious.

"Gwey-gwey!" Okwaho called, alerting them to his presence.

The woman standing between the two men turned. It was his mother, Wolf Woman. And as soon as she saw him, the look of worry on her face turned into a smile.

"My son," Wolf Woman called, opening her arms and looking up at the sky in a gesture of thanks.

She stepped quickly forward as Okwaho crossed the distance between the trail head and the stockade.

Wolf Woman reached him before he arrived at the opening. Burnt Hair, Holds the Door Open, and several other men, all of them holding bows and arrows, had come out to stand close behind them. They said nothing, but they looked grim.

As his mother embraced him, Okwaho saw through the entrance into the stockade a woman coming out of the Snipe Clan longhouse. She stopped to stand unmoving in front of the door. Her name was Bird Flying and she was the mother of Tawis. The look on her face— seeing Okwaho alone without her son—was not one of joy.

Tawis, Okwaho thought.

Immediately, all the pain he'd been holding back flooded his heart. Tawis, his best friend. They had been friends since they'd been able to take their first steps. It was Tawis who, at the age of only two winters, walked over to him as he sat outside by the fire and smiled at him. Then Tawis had handed him a ball.

His mother saw the distress in his face. She leaned over and took him gently by the arm.

"Was it Atatarho?" she asked. "Has he finally decided to . . ."

"No." Okwaho said. "Enemies . . . enemies surprised us as we were fishing. They were Standing Stone People, Oneidas. Just three of them. They know where our village is. And they captured Tawis and I . . . I . . ." His voice choked and he could not say more.

"You escaped," his mother whispered into his ear. She held him for a time without speaking, then she loosened her embrace.

She turned to look at Okwaho's father. He and four of the strongest and fastest men in the village had now gathered near the gate. They'd heard what Okwaho said. It was clear they'd made a plan quickly to go in pursuit of the Standing Stone war party.

But Holds the Door Open and the four other men stood there waiting. A decision such as this could not be made by men alone. In their little breakaway village where there were no elders, Wolf Woman had become the head clan mother. Did she agree?

She held up both hands and swung them toward the woods. As one, the men turned and began running, disappearing onto the forest trail. If they were lucky—or unlucky, for when there was fighting someone always would get hurt—they might catch up with the raiding party before night. Though their village was devoted to avoiding aggression, seeking to rescue someone just taken captive was a different thing. If they caught up to the Standing Stone party, perhaps there would be no fight. Faced by an equal or larger force of strong men— they might just release their captive and retreat.

Even in these days when fighting seemed to be everywhere, it was the job of any man leading a raiding party to keep his men safe. Losing even one man in battle was a disgraceful thing.

If only I could go with them, Okwaho thought, feeling the anger building inside him like a tightly clenched fist. *I would strike them hard!*

Wolf Woman gently pulled him back.

"Come," she said. "You need to tell Bird Flying what happened to her son."

She stayed by his side as they walked back to the entrance to the stockade. As soon as they passed through the door, two young men named Fox Tail and

Chases Rabbits closed the opening with the strongly made gate that they propped firmly into place.

Okwaho looked around. It seemed that all of the rest of the ten handfuls of people who made up their little community were looking at him. They had come out of their longhouses or were already in the central area between them all. People of his own Wolf Clan had come from their longhouse, those of the Turtle Clan, the Deer Clan, and Tawis's Snipe Clan had emerged from theirs. Not all of the clans of the Onondagas, the Among the Hills Nation, were represented here in the village where people had chosen to try to live in peace. Especially not the Bear Clan. That clan was headed by Atatarho, the Entangled One, the huge man who had become the great war chief of the Onondaga Nation. The one they were free from—for now.

No one had as much power as Atatarho did—either physically or in terms of spiritual strength. He seemed to embody an enraged bear, striking out against anyone within reach who dared get in his way. Like everyone, he had lost friends and relatives to the endless cycle of war. But no one was as twisted by that experience as Atatarho. Even his body was bent over and twisted from carrying that huge weight of anger.

"We will kill them," he would growl. "We will destroy all those who try to stand against us."

Angry and vengeful, Atatarho no longer listened to the advice of the clan mothers. His power was always directed toward conflict and war. And so the families from those four clans had left to find peace and safety.

But we were not really safe, Okwaho thought as he kicked at the ground while they walked. *All we were was foolish.*

Bird Flying, the mother of his friend, had not moved from her place in front of her longhouse.

"Go to her," Wolf Woman whispered.

Taking a deep breath, Okwaho approached Bird Flying.

He opened his mouth, uncertain of what to say other than how sorry he was, but she raised a hand.

"Just tell me," she said. "Tell me what my son did. Tell me why you are here and he is not."

Okwaho felt his mother's hand on his shoulder.

"We were fishing," he said. His own words sounded hollow to him as he spoke them. "We thought it was safe. But they were on us before we knew it. There were three of them. They caught Tawis. But he helped me so I could get away."

"And what did Tawis do to help you escape?" Bird Flying asked. The fact that her voice was so kind—despite the pain he saw in her eyes—made it hard for Okwaho to reply. Bird Flying was always kind, no matter what. Even after her husband, Looks Forward, had been killed—back before they left Onondaga to make this small village—she never expressed anger toward the Swampy Land People whose warriors had killed him.

Okwaho took another breath. "Tawis," he said, "my friend, my brother, he shouted 'RUN!' Then he dove at the men and knocked them into the stream."

A very small smile came to the lips of Bird Flying. "Of course." She nodded. "That is my son. And you did as he wanted. You got away."

Okwaho nodded. "Maybe he'll find some way to escape," he said. It was all he could think to say. And even as he spoke those words it seemed as if he was hearing someone else say them, someone who was unsure of himself and did not believe what he was saying.

"Perhaps he may," Bird Flying said, but there was no hope in her voice.

How could she have any hope? Okwaho thought. *How can any of us have hope for anything?*

Every person in their little village had lost someone over the last few years. A brother, a father, an uncle killed in war. A sister, a brother, a dear friend, or even a mother, taken away, kidnapped to become part of another nation. There they might take the place and even the name of another person lost from that other nation as a result of the war that had no end. It made Okwaho angry to think about it. This endless warfare was like a cannibal monster that was always hungry, always reaching out with its skeletal hands to take more and more lives.

Bird Flying looked toward the direction from which Okwaho had come running. It was not as if she was trying to see anything or anyone. It was as if she was saying goodbye. Then she sighed, turned, and went back into the Snipe Clan longhouse.

chapter three
STORY

A story is a powerful thing. When he was only five winters old, Okwaho had asked his mother why stories had such an effect, why whenever he heard one told he felt as if he was there while the story was happening. Even when it was a tale from long ago, or one about such monsters as stone giants and talking heads, it was as if it was happening right before him, taking place all around him. He no longer heard his mother's voice. Instead he found himself seeing and experiencing things alongside the ones the story was about.

What was just as amazing was that it was the same for the other children gathered around and listening. Each of them felt as if she or he was the one the story was about—the three hunters driving the great bear up into the sky land, the little girl who knew how to defeat the cannibal giant, even the rabbit managing to trick the wildcat that wanted to eat it. Okwaho knew this was true. He had asked the other children how they felt during the stories' telling—especially Tawis and Clouds Forming.

Although she was the youngest daughter of Grows Corn, the head of the society of women planters, his friend Clouds Forming had little interest in farming. Because everyone knew it was important to allow children to choose their own path, her mother never forced her to go to the fields to care for the Three Sisters—the Corn, the Beans, and the Squash—with the other girls. So there was no problem when Clouds Forming chose to play with Tawis and Okwaho. Strong as any boy and a faster runner than most, she was fearless when groups of children played tewaraathon. Everyone stepped out of her way when she swung her stick to catch or throw the ball. Okwaho and Tawis enjoyed the way she always challenged them. It made them try even harder and get even better at every physical activity they shared.

Though the same age, Clouds Forming was a hand taller than Okwaho and just as strong. She could throw a spear as far and as accurately as boys who were winters older than her. Whenever the three of them wrestled, she won at least as often as either of the two boys. Then, when she had tripped or thrown one of them to the earth, she would sit on the chest of whomever she'd thrown to the ground, their dogs circling them and barking with excitement.

"You," she would say, her voice mock serious as she poked her vanquished opponent—usually Okwaho—in the chest with her finger, "you are going to have to grow stronger if you ever expect me to choose you for a husband. I will not bake marriage bread and take it to the mother of a weakling."

Then, she would hop up, grab Okwaho's hand, and laugh as she pulled him to his feet.

People joked about them being triplets or sewn together with an invisible cord, for they did almost everything together and seemed to feel the same way about everything. The three of them were like kernels from the same ear of corn.

"How do you feel when a story is being told?" Okwaho had asked each of his friends in turn.

"What do you mean?" Tawis asked. "I feel the warmth of the fire. I feel the deerskin underneath me. And sometimes I feel cool air on my back when someone opens the door flap of the longhouse."

Clouds Forming laughed and slapped Tawis playfully on his arm. "Stop being silly," she said. "You know what Okwaho means." Then she answered his question herself. "While we were listening to that story your mother just shared, I felt as if I was flying to the sky land along with Turkey Buzzard to bring back clothes for all the other birds. And I know you felt that way too,

Tawis." She lifted her hand as if to swat Tawis a second time and he scooted back from her.

"Do not hit me again," he said, making his voice small like that of a little child. "You are going to break my arm, you bully! You should be called Lightning Striking, not Clouds Forming."

Then Tawis grinned at Okwaho. "My friend, sometimes you are sooo serious," he said. "But Clouds Forming is right. She is right twice. First, I was teasing you. Second, I always feel as if I am no longer inside our longhouse listening to a story. I feel as if I am part of the story. When that one was done, I had to look at my arms to make sure I was not covered with brown feathers like Turkey Buzzard."

Okwaho had gone to his mother after that conversation with his two friends.

"I have a question," he said.

"You always do," his mother replied. Then she smiled. "And I am always ready to try to answer you. Though I still cannot explain to you why water is wet and fire is hot."

"It is about stories," Okwaho said, choosing not to laugh at his mother's teasing. "Why are they so strong? Why do your stories always take me somewhere?"

"Ah," Wolf Woman said. "You are finally asking me an easy question, Okwaho. Stories are so strong because they are alive. A story is like someone you trust to take your hand, lead you on a journey, and then bring you back home again."

Okwaho had nodded at that answer. It had made it easier for him to understand why he and his friends felt as they did, not just during a story but after one had been told. It was as if they had been guided along a trail, sometimes one they'd traveled before and sometimes a new one, guided by someone like his mother or his uncle, someone who cared about them, showed them wonderful things along the way, and then brought them back to their longhouse safe and happy.

Okwaho shook his head as he sat with his back against his mother's longhouse. His best friend was gone. His other friend Clouds Forming was back in Onondaga and perhaps he would never see her again. Nothing made sense without them. What use was a story now?

As Okwaho looked down, he saw a stone on the ground. He picked it up and hefted it. It was round and heavy, the size of one of the balls they used to play tewaraathon. It was the perfect size for throwing. It made him think again of Clouds Forming.

She had always teased Okwaho about being stronger than he was, so that she could always throw a stone farther. It almost made him smile when he remembered that, for it was true. And he had never minded her being better than him at anything. He'd always enjoyed being around her, and that enjoyment had only become greater as they'd grown older.

In fact, now that each of the friends had three handfuls of winters, Clouds Forming had become a good-looking young woman. And she was well aware of that.

"Before long," she would sometimes say to Okwaho and Tawis, "it will be time for me to choose a man to be my husband. To which of your mothers shall I bring marriage bread? Or should I just marry you both? I have no doubt that both of your mothers would gladly give you to me. After all, who would she ever want who was better than me?"

All three of them had laughed at her gentle teasing. But the truth of it was that neither Tawis nor Okwaho would have minded a grown-up life where the three of them would always be together.

She had wanted to come with them. But her family had chosen not to join the new village. As close relatives of Atatarho, how could they?

So, for the first time in their lives, the three young people had been separated. Okwaho and Tawis were sad about many things involved in moving away from their familiar lives, but their separation from Clouds Forming made them saddest.

It was Clouds Forming whom they saw last as they left the village among the hills. She had been standing by the opening of the huge stockade wall encircling the entire village. She had waved at them until they could no longer see her after turning onto the trail through the grove of maple trees.

chapter four
THE MORNING

Okwaho lay on the sleeping rack against the southern wall of their longhouse. He did not want to rise. The constant burning of anger within him was not being cured by sleep. Whenever he did sleep, it gave him no rest. Either he found himself reliving the loss of his friend, trying to find a way for Tawis to escape, or he saw himself as a grown man, a well-armed warrior setting out to take revenge. But in those dreams of vengeance he never succeeded. He always woke before he could strike their enemies, staring up at the smoke hole in the longhouse roof.

Then he had listened to the sounds of the others in their family compartments along either wall of the Wolf Clan longhouse. On the rack below him, his father—who'd returned unsuccessful from the attempt to catch the raiders—and his mother had slept almost as fitfully as he did. Only Okwaho's little sister, snuggled in between them, had seemed to truly be resting.

I will go back to sleep, he'd silently said to himself each time he woke. *This time when I dream, Tawis and I will escape. And when I wake up in the morning he will be standing by my sleeping rack, tickling me. Or maybe pouring a dipper of water over my head.*

But each time the same thing happened. Tawis was captured as Okwaho ran. He would wake biting his lip, trying not to shout his lost friend's name. Again and again and again it went on that way.

Why must I be only a boy, he thought. *Why can I not be a grown man? One who can do something meaningful!*

He reached one arm down to scoop up a handful of kernels of dried corn from the elm bark basket by his bed. It was the last of the corn saved from the harvest of the year before.

"Corn," he whispered, "can you help me? Bring me a song to take my thoughts to a better place?"

Okwaho began to let kernels fall, one by one, from one hand into the other and back again. The whisper and rattle of one grain against another sounded like a voice. Like the rhythm of a song. So many things always made him think of songs—old ones and ones that wanted to enter his thoughts. Even now when anger was twisting in his head, the songs were still there waiting for him. Like the one coming to him now.

He took a breath and began to sing.

Corn, I thank you.
Corn, I thank you.
You and your two sisters
Bring us life.

And as he sang, a story came into his mind—the oldest story his people knew, the tale of how this earth came to be.

Long ago, a woman fell from the sky. She brought with her seeds from the sky tree. The water creatures had prepared a place for her by putting soil onto the back of the Great Turtle as it floated on the surface of the ocean. She let those seeds fall into her tracks in the moist earth as she danced with small steps—as the women of the five Longhouse Nations dance to this day.

Sky Woman had a daughter, the first human born on this earth. And when her daughter was grown, she married the west wind and gave birth to two sons. And that was when all the trouble began. For one of those boys was kind and generous. The other was angry and selfish and deceitful. They were called the Good Mind and Flint. The Good Mind was born in the normal way, but Flint thrust himself out through his mother's side, killing her.

The two of them began to struggle over who would control the world. The Good Mind made fruits and flowers. Flint made thorns and poisonous plants. The Good Mind made rivers that flowed gently. Flint made rapids and threw in big stones that would sink canoes. The Good Mind made all kinds of fish that were good to eat. Flint made monsters that hid underwater waiting to drag people in and eat them. So it went until finally the two of them wrestled. When the Good Mind won, Flint, the twisted-minded one, was banished.

But the Twisted Mind is not totally gone.

At times, Flint is able to influence our thoughts toward selfishness and anger. But the Good Mind is always there to guide us back toward peace and sharing.

Okwaho sat up, still holding the kernels of corn in his hand. It was a good song and a good story that the corn had brought to him. For a moment, that moment as he was singing and seeing that story happen, the anger had almost left him. It was that way when he thought of peace.

Only a few generations ago, according to his mother, the five sister nations of the Haudenosaunee, the Longhouse People, had lived together in peace. They had all been following the way of the Good Mind. But that was no longer true. Now, with the endless cycle of raid and counter-raid, of attack and revenge, the balance had tipped toward Flint. Men such as Atatarho, who no longer listened to the Good Mind, were in charge.

Okwaho shook his head. Neither the song nor the story had really helped him at all.

He pushed the elm bark basket of corn aside. It was the fourth morning since his escape from the Oneida raiding party. Sleep had not come easily. Whenever he did sleep, his dreams kept taking him back to the events of the day before.

The longhouse was empty aside from him. Everyone else had gone about their daily chores. His parents had let him sleep. They had to have noticed his restlessness all through the night. But they had not disturbed him. What good would it have done?

A pot of corn mush hung over the cooking fire in the center of the longhouse. He took the wooden spoon that hung by a rawhide string from his belt and dipped into the hot mush.

"Thank you for this food," he said. Then he blew on the spoonful of mush to cool it, before putting it into his mouth. It had been sweetened with maple sugar. Not only did it taste good, he realized how hungry he was. He took another, bigger spoonful and then another. He felt starved as a wolf in winter. But as he was filling his stomach, the thought of Tawis came back to him.

It hit him like a blow to his head. Where was his

friend now? Was he well or suffering? Was he eating or being starved by his captors? The corn mush no longer tasted as good to him. He licked his spoon clean, wiped it with a corn husk, and put it back onto his belt. He dipped one of the nearby gourds into the clay pot beaded with sweat that sat a long arm's length from the fire. "Thank you," he said. Then he washed down the last of his breakfast with the cool spring water.

When he stepped outside, there were few of his fellow villagers to be seen. The sun was already two hands above the horizon. By now most of the women had gone down the hill to the fields, accompanied by well-armed men to guard them while they worked. Burnt Hair was standing watchfully by the village gate, and Okwaho's father had stationed himself by the edge of the main path into the woods.

Okwaho was relieved to see his father and Tawis's uncle. He understood what that meant. If there was a raid planned on the Oneidas, they would have been the ones to lead it. Despite what had happened, they were not going off on a raid of their own to seek revenge.

A little group of small children were playing the hoop game by the southern wall of the palisade around their town. But he didn't see . . .

A stone formed in his belly as Okwaho realized what he was doing. He was looking around for Tawis as he

always did each day. Expecting his best friend—the
only young person of his age who had ended up in their
small community—to creep up and jump on him from
behind to start one of their wrestling matches that often
ended with neither being able to throw the other.

Okwaho started walking toward the gate. He nodded
at his father and then at Burnt Hair, but said nothing.
He didn't even speak the morning greeting—"I am glad
to see you looking well."

His father, seeming to understand that words were
not possible, or perhaps that silence might communicate
more than words at a time such as this, also said nothing. He only nodded and squeezed his son's shoulder
gently as he walked through the gate. Okwaho went no
farther than the edge of the woods, where he relieved
himself and then turned to look back.

To the side of their longhouse, his mother, Wolf
Woman, was pounding corn in a mortar not far from
the group of playing children. She lifted her chin, beck-
oning him toward her.

Okwaho walked across the village center to sit next
to her. Neither of them spoke. He leaned back against
the stockade wall and listened. The drumbeat sound
of the corn being pounded was soothing, like that of a
song so old, it could no longer be translated into human
speech. She stopped to pour out the finely ground corn

from the mortar into a bowl. Okwaho poured more kernels of corn into the mortar and his mother began using the pestle again.

When the last of the corn had been pounded, she wiped her hands on her dress and sat down next to him.

"How did things come to be this way?" Okwaho asked.

"It has happened before," Wolf Woman replied.

chapter five
MESSENGERS

Okwaho's mother began the story called "The Twins."

"Long ago," his mother said, "Teharonhia:wako, The one Who Grasps the Sky with Both Hands, the right-handed twin, the Good-Minded One, sent a messenger to give instructions to the first human beings. Hoh?"

"Henh," Okwaho replied, showing he was truly listening.

"Those instructions were not hard. That first messenger explained that all we human beings needed to do was remember to always give thanks. To help us do this, we were taught the words to be spoken before all others. With those words, we could carefully greet and thank all parts of Creation before beginning any important task. Although many seem to have forgotten this—such as Atatarho—we must remember those words."

"Henh," Okwaho said.

Wolf Woman nodded and then began to speak those Thanksgiving words.

"We greet and thank our Mother, the Earth, the one who gave birth to us and who cares for all life.

"We greet and thank the waters, the rivers and streams, the lakes, and the water that flows through our own bodies.

"We greet and thank the trees, especially the maple, who is the leader of all the trees and is the first to give us a harvest in the form of its sweet sap.

"We greet and thank all of the plants that teach us and allow us to use their roots and stems, their leaves and flowers, as medicine.

"We greet and thank the Three Sisters, those who sustain us by providing us with food, the Corn, the Beans, the Squash . . ."

His mother, her eyes raised as she spoke, continued through the list of all the gifts of life, acknowledging the animals, the birds, the winds, the Moon, the Sun, the Stars. Okwaho nodded again and again. It always calmed his insides, made his breath slow and even. His heart felt a little less burdened by care and anger as he heard the Thanksgiving words spoken.

"Then," Wolf Woman said, "we greet and thank all of the People, those we know, those we have not yet met. And we thank our Creator, who has brought all of this into being."

She took a long slow breath and turned her gaze to her son. "Okwaho, because I am only a human being, I may have forgotten some who should be thanked, so I ask you to think of them and add your own thanks."

"Henh," Okwaho said.

"It was good to do this, it is still good to this day," Wolf Woman said. "Hoh?"

"Henh."

"As I said at the end of those thanks, we humans are weak and forgetful. We are not like our wiser relatives, the animal people who always remember their place in Creation and their proper role. As a result, long ago, a time came when we humans began to forget those words to be spoken. The people back then no longer gave thanks. They began to quarrel and fight with each other. As so many of us are doing now."

Okwaho nodded. It was painfully true.

His mother lifted her right hand toward the Sky World. "But The One Who Grasps the Sky with Both Hands saw this. So a second messenger was sent. This one brought us ceremonies that would remind us of our place in the world and that we were part of a great Creation."

She paused, placed her hand on Okwaho's knee and squeezed it gently.

"You know those ceremonies, for we still have them. There is one each season, the Midwinter Festival, the

Thanks to the Maple Festival, the Planting Festival, the Green Corn Festival, and all the others. Our people were also given the Clan system. Turtle, Bear, Wolf, for all of our Five Nations, as well as Snipe, Deer, Eel, Heron, Beaver, and Hawk for our Onondaga people. Each clan would be headed by a clan mother and the people were reminded that the women are the ones from whom all life and all power comes. Each child belongs to the clan of her or his mother. And the clan mothers would be the ones who choose the leaders, who decide if the nation can go to war, who must be consulted in all important matters. Also, the clans linked our Five Nations together. If an Onondaga person is of the Bear Clan, then those in the other four nations who are also Bear Clan are to be seen as your sisters and brothers."

Wolf Woman paused, looking at Okwaho.

"And then the people forgot again?" he said.

His mother nodded. "And that is how it is now. The minds of our leaders have become twisted. They no longer think first of giving thanks, first of peace. They no longer turn to the clan mothers for guidance. Instead, they think only of power, of making war and striking back at those who strike us. And the Entangled One, Atatarho, is the worst of all. That is why we left our place among the hills and came here to form the village of Kanata."

Wolf Woman sighed and sat there silently.

Finally, Okwaho broke the silence. Unlike the story he'd remembered when he first woke, this one had been like a ray of hope, pushing back the darkness of his anger. Things had been bad before and then good had come to the people. Perhaps, just perhaps, it was time for that to happen again.

"I think," he said in a firm voice, "The One Who Grasps the Sky with Both Hands needs to send another messenger."

"My son," his mother said, "I think you are right."

chapter six
GAUNTLET

Ten sunrises had passed since the Standing Stone raiding party. Although no attack had been made yet on Kanata and their scouts had seen no sign of any enemies, everyone knew how much danger they were in. Before they had been worried that Atatarho would change his mind and send warriors to force them back to Onondaga. But now they had other enemies to worry about. Doubt had set in about what they should do now. So they had called a council meeting.

As it had always been among the Longhouse people—or at least as it had always been before Atatarho took his place as the only voice that counted—every adult had been allowed their say. Every woman and man had been listened to carefully. Questions were asked.

What will we do when another raiding party comes? Do we have enough men to defend our small village?

Would it be better to be back at Onondaga?

Should we try to move our village again?

Should we return to Onondaga?

Finally a decision was made that everyone agreed upon. A delegation should be sent to try to speak with Atatarho. If he agreed to listen to them, they could find out if it was possible for them to return. If he said that no return was possible, then at least they would not be wasting their time trying to decide whether to stay or return. If their nest no longer exists, birds cannot go back to it.

Burnt Hair and Holds the Door Open were ready. They had been chosen to carry just that one question.

If we wished to return, could we do so?

It was just before dawn. As the two men left the village, they did not notice they were not alone.

Okwaho had learned the lessons taught him by his uncle and his father well.

To follow someone, he'd been told, *you do not need to keep them in sight. You do not even need to hear them. Follow the signs of their passing. Or, even better, if you know where they are going, set out for that place circling around them.*

After half a day's walk, Burnt Hair and Holds the Door Open reached the beginning of the main trail that led to the big village. Okwaho was close enough now to see them far below him, having circled ahead as his uncle had taught. He was just beyond where the sentries of the big village were usually posted. His hiding place, in a small tree near the base of the highest hill around Onondaga, was close enough for him to see and hear whatever might happen. His heart was beating fast. How would they be greeted—as friends or as traitors who had deserted the big village?

He watched as his father and Burnt Hair took their first steps onto that well-traveled path to the big village. Before they had taken a handful of steps, seven armed warriors stepped out from behind the tall pine trees along the path. Even from his hiding place, Okwaho's eyes were keen enough to recognize them. Those warriors were people that Burnt Hair and Holds the Door Open knew well. Some of them had been their friends. But the arrows pointed at them were not a sign of welcoming. A tall man with a scar that ran from his chin to his right ear stepped forward from behind the men with bows. He lifted up a heavy war club threateningly. Okwaho knew him, even though his face was painted black. It was Over the Creek, a member of the Turtle Clan. He had often gone hunting with Okwaho's father.

Holds the Door Open and Burnt Hair held out their empty hands.

"We have no weapons," Burnt Hair said.

"Then you are fools," Over the Creek replied in a harsh voice.

"We wish to speak to Atatarho," Holds the Door Open said.

"You wish to see our Great Chief? That is a foolish wish," Over the Creek said. His voice sounded amused now.

Another man holding a long spear stepped forward. His face was also painted black, but he was just as easy to recognize. Shorter and broader than Over the Creek, he was named On the Watch. A member of Atatarho's own Bear Clan, he was one of the great chief's counselors.

"We will bring them to our Great Chief," On the Watch said. "We will enjoy hearing what he has to say to them after they have finished speaking."

"I will run ahead," Over the Creek said.

On the Watch nodded. He watched as Over the Creek turned and began running as fast as he could. He watched until Over the Creek had vanished from sight around a bend in the trail.

On the Watch lifted his left hand and swung it around. The remaining men formed a circle around the two messengers. On the Watch prodded Burnt Hair and Holds the Door Open with the butt of his spear.

"Run," he said.

The eight men, the two delegates and the six warriors encircling them, began to run. Not as fast as Over the Creek had been running, but at a quick trot, through the hills and down into the valley.

Staying back where he could not be seen, Okwaho followed. He knew what he was doing was foolish. If any of those warriors heard him, the first thing they might do would be to shoot their arrows in his direction. They might even kill his father and Burnt Hair, thinking that they had been deceived and that a raiding party was sneaking up on them.

I should turn back, Okwaho thought. But he did not.

No further words were spoken, even as the Onondaga warriors and their two prisoners ran past the main gate. They took the small, winding trail that led up and to the left of the palisaded village where more than a thousand people lived in the nine clan longhouses. Wolf, Turtle, Beaver, Snipe, Heron, Deer, Eel, Bear, and Hawk.

Okwaho knew where the trail they were on was leading. They were heading to Atatarho's Rock.

The big stone that thrust itself out of the earth in a large clearing was where Atatarho sat whenever he called a council meeting or had anyone brought before him. At that place he made the decisions that brought life to some and death to others.

Okwaho began to feel a little hopeful when he

realized that that was where his father and Burnt Hair were being taken. It meant their message would be listened to.

But, he thought, *it might also mean that they will be killed there.*

Sure enough, just as expected, when they reached the clearing Atatarho was there, seated on his great, long stone. But he did not turn to look at them. His gaze was toward the wide waters of Onondaga Lake, which could be seen behind him. Nothing moved on the lake. Not a bird or a wave.

Atatarho's face was as expressionless as the rock itself. He gave no sign that he was aware of their arrival as the two men came to a stop before the stone. Then Atatarho turned his head toward them. His dark eyes stared at them with a gaze like that of a monster bear about to leap on its prey and tear it apart. The men who had escorted them there stepped quickly away and moved to stand on either side of the most powerful of all the Longhouse Nation chiefs, who continued to stare down at the two messengers.

It was quiet there in the clearing. No wind was blowing, no birds were singing. There were no sounds of insects in the grass. All that could be heard was two things. The first was the heavy, slow breathing of the giant of a man who looked down his nose at them. The second thing they heard was the incessant hissing of the black snakes tied into Atatarho's long, thick hair. He paid no attention to them, even though they were constantly trying to escape, thrusting their heads forward and then coiling back again and again and again.

The sight of those snakes alone was often enough to make anyone brought before the Great Chief tremble and fall to their knees. Yet Burnt Hair and Holds the Door Open knew Atatarho and stood before him with straight backs. Okwaho felt proud of the way they stood there. They were keeping their gaze on the ground below Atatarho's feet—for that was always the polite thing to do. But they showed no sign of fear or weakness.

The silence stretched on for so long that Okwaho began to hear a third sound—that of his own heart beating—so loud, he was afraid it would give away his position where he was crouched down in the tall ferns that covered the hillside leading down to the lake.

"Speak," Atatarho roared. His deep, angry voice echoed throughout the clearing so loudly that Okwaho almost jumped.

"Standing Stone men came and stole one of our boys," Burnt Hair said. "They have found our little village. We now know that we are no longer safe in our new place."

"Hah! You think I do not know this?" Atatarho replied, his voice filled with contempt. "I know all things that happen. The birds and the wind carry messages to me. Every animal in the forest brings me word of the things that come to pass."

He looked for a moment toward the place where Okwaho was hiding and the ghost of a smile curled his lips.

"We do not doubt this," Holds the Door Open said. "We did not come here to tell you that. We held a meeting and it was decided to send us as messengers to ask you a question."

Atatarho said nothing at first. He just sat there on his judgment rock, staring at them so intently that it seemed to Okwaho he was staring inside them. The men who had brought them to the Great Chief waited on either side of the rock, war clubs held across their bodies. If Atatarho gave the signal, Okwaho did not doubt that those men would step forward and beat both the messengers to death. He remembered the story of what had happened to the envoys from the Swampy Land People two moons before he and his family and the others left the big village.

Four messengers from the Swampy Land People had come to beg the Great Chief of the Onondagas not to raid them any longer.

We will give you anything you ask of us. Food, baskets, canoes, anything we make. We only ask to be allowed enough to live, the Swampy Land spokesman had pleaded. *Take one out of four of our women and our children. Only leave enough of us so that we may survive as a people.*

Hah, Atatarho had laughed. *What enjoyment will there be in that for us? Why do you think your offer means anything? We are strong and can take whatever we want from you, you who are as weak as rabbits. We, who are wolves, we will come whenever we decide. If you do not fight us—as we wish you to—we will just kill all of your men and take your women and children to be ours. They will die—just as three of you will die now.*

Then he had made a fist and waved it at the three Swampy Land men behind the man who had stepped forward to speak. Without hesitation, his bodyguards had raised their clubs and leaped upon the unarmed Swampy Land messengers, killing those three and leaving only the spokesman who had begged for peace.

Now, Atatarho had said to the shocked survivor, *carry my message back to your people.*

The memory of what had been done to those pitiful Swampy Land messengers was the reason that only Holds the Door Open and Burnt Hair had been sent to speak to Atatarho. If his decision was to kill, leaving one alive to carry back his message, then just one man would die.

Burnt Hair and Holds the Door Open stood there, backs still straight, waiting for the cruel chief to break the silence. The midday heat from Elder Brother Sun beat down upon them. Okwaho could see beads of sweat running down their foreheads.

Atatarho's men also waited, looking down at their own feet. Over the Creek, the tall, scarred man who had been close to both of them, was trying to show no emotion, but the way he kept sucking in his lips showed Okwaho that the thought of killing one of his former friends must be troubling him.

Then Atatarho leaned over and smiled down at them. It was a smile that held no kindness. It was more like the expression on the face of a bear as it shows its teeth before attacking.

"Ask your question," he said, his voice as deep and ominous as a roll of thunder.

Holds the Door Open took a step forward, hands held out before him with his palms up.

"If we abandon our new village and return to Onondaga, what will happen?"

Atatarho laughed. His laugh was like the roar of a fierce beast, filling the clearing. It was so loud and threatening that the men holding their clubs to either side of him flinched. But neither Holds the Door Open nor Burnt Hair moved. They stood there, eyes looking down at the earth, still showing respect, but not displaying the fear both of them felt at that moment.

They know, Okwaho thought, a shiver running down his back like an icy drop of rain, *that if they show either weakness or defiance now, it may be the end of them both.*

"Hah!" Atatarho growled. "You want to know what my answer would be if you asked to return?" He paused. Neither Burnt Hair nor Holds the Door Open said anything. What he'd just said was not a question.

Atatarho leaned forward, his right hand held up, his index finger pointing at the ground. "It will be easy," he said. "Just come here and run the gauntlet. That way I will know you are worthy to be part of Onondaga again."

Running the gauntlet. Okwaho understood what that meant, even though he had never seen it. It was an old way of testing the bravery of men taken captive. People, sometimes everyone in a village, would make two lines facing inward. In their hands they would hold sticks. Those who had to prove themselves would run between those two lines of people holding sticks, being struck on both sides by everyone they passed. Sometimes, the blows struck would be light ones, especially when the person being tested was a young man worthy of adoption. At the end of the line his new family members would be waiting with open arms to welcome him as one of them. Also, if someone showed particular bravery, walking through the gauntlet rather than running, those holding the sticks might just reach out and touch him with their sticks as he passed by them.

Other times, though, the blows struck in the gauntlet would be brutal ones, hard enough to bruise, to draw blood. Some who ran the gauntlet never made it through. They would fall and be beaten to death.

Hearing that running the gauntlet would be their only test almost made Burnt Hair and Holds the Door Open smile. The men of their little breakaway village could surely endure that.

But Atatarho was not finished.

One of the snakes in his hair had wriggled free and had started to crawl down his massive shoulder. Atatarho reached over and grasped the black snake with his left hand. It flicked its tongue out at him as he held it up in front of him.

"Yes," Atatarho said, as if having heard the snake speak to him. "Yes."

He dropped the snake and watched as it slithered down into a hole beneath the great rock where he sat.

Atatarho pointed his finger straight at the two men. "All of you who left me will have to do this. Men, women, children, old people. All fifty of you will run the gauntlet. All of you must come as one. If any person from your group of cowards and fools is missing when they return, everyone will be shot with arrows."

Burnt Hair was biting his lip to keep himself from speaking. Holds the Door Open was drawing in a deep breath in an effort to remain silent.

Atatarho sat back and grinned again, folding his hands over his chest and nodding his head. He pointed with his chin to the right and the left to indicate his bodyguards. "Further, the gauntlet will be made up of men such as these. One hundred of them. And they will not be holding little sticks. They will have heavy clubs and they will strike hard!"

Atatarho laughed, a laugh in which there was no trace of humor. "I will give you some time to consider my generous offer. But if you do not all return here by the end of two moons, then I may just send my warriors to destroy you and your pathetic little village."

Atatarho opened his hands and swung them forward as if shooing away flies. "Now go. For now I spare you." The terrible smile returned to his face as he pointed his chin toward the place where Okwaho still hid. "All three of you."

Neither Holds the Door Open nor Burnt Hair said a word as Okwaho joined them at the head of the trail that led from Onondaga. Nor did any of them speak on the journey back to their small village. But they placed him in between them as they walked. And when they were within sight of their home, his father reached out and put his arm around Okwaho's shoulders.

chapter seven
SOMETHING USEFUL

The visit of the two messengers to Atatarho had not made things better. When Holds the Door Open and Burnt Hair had related what happened to the gathering of everyone in their peaceful village, the shock that everyone felt was like a blow from one of those clubs in the gauntlet. There could be no return. They were truly on their own. If anything, their mission to speak with the cruel chief had just made things worse. If they did go back to Onondaga, none of them might survive the gauntlet. But if they stayed in Kanata, after the passage of two moons Atatarho might still send his warriors to attack them.

Okwaho shook his head and opened his eyes to another day. No matter how long he stayed in bed, nothing would be different. His best friend would still be gone. And their small village, even though they had tried to find peace, was no longer safe.

He thought again about the decision he and Tawis made that day—to go out, just the two of them, to the stream. Had it been his idea or Tawis's? Like so many things they did together—used to do together—it had been as if they were one mind in complete agreement. They hardly had to speak to know what their plans were that day. Go fishing.

As always, their mothers had not forbidden them to go out beyond the safety of their little walled village. After all, they knew, as did every mother of their nation, that to tell a young person not to do something could have the opposite result. To forbid a child any course of action might waken that small voice within that would eventually lead to their doing the thing they were told not to do.

To go fishing would be safe. That was what they'd foolishly believed. Without the voice of Atatarho constantly urging his young men to go and raid their enemies, they'd imagined that war would not touch them. They would have peace in their new village. The two of them could venture out on their own and not be in danger.

What a fool I was! Okwaho thought. *Believing in peace?*

He felt the anger in him growing again. Anger at himself as well as at those who took his best friend from him. And as the anger grew, the face of Atatarho came into his mind. A man so filled with anger that it twisted his body. Was that how he would eventually look?

Okwaho shook his head. The anger inside him was like a spiderweb, trapping his thoughts. He wiped his face with the palms of his hands. Enough! He had to do something.

He swung his legs out over the edge of his sleeping rack and dropped lightly to the floor of the longhouse. He unhooked his wooden spoon from his belt, where it always hung connected by a rawhide cord with a toggle at the end of it.

Okwaho knelt by the cooking pot, dipped out a spoonful of venison soup, and ate it. In addition to the deer meat there was corn and beans and squash mixed in, along with the seasoning of salt and dried sassafras leaves ground and stirred into the stew to thicken it. He also tasted the hint of sweetness from the maple sugar his mother sometimes added. The soup was warm and good and he felt its warmth in his throat and then his belly. Good food was truly a medicine. For a moment it almost made him forget his anger and regret. Almost.

He ate more of the soup, feeling the strength of the deer that had given its life enter his own body, feeling the love that his mother put into every meal that she prepared. Perhaps his father was out hunting right now, seeking more game to sustain them. And his mother was surely doing something useful as well. Perhaps she was smoke-tanning a deerskin or working on a pair of moccasins.

While he, Okwaho, was doing nothing for anyone.

What could he do to be useful?

The stockade wall, that was it. He'd heard Burnt Hair talking about how it needed to be reinforced on the side toward the sunrise.

He poured some water into his spoon from the clay pot set off to the side and drank it. He wiped his spoon dry with the corner of his loin cloth and then stuck the toggle back under his belt.

It was a bright day. Elder Brother Sun was giving his warmth gladly to the earth. Okwaho smelled the scent of the smoke from fire across the compound where his mother and some of the other women were sitting next to a set of racks where deerskins were drying. He nodded at his mother, who nodded back to him before going back to her task of softening deerskin by chewing it before stitching it into the uppers of moccasins. Bird Flying, the mother of Tawis, was there too. She did not look up at him. She almost never looked at him now.

Okwaho bit his lip and continued walking. Three men were working on preparing a post to be added to the stockade wall. One of them was Burnt Hair. Okwaho went over to them. He didn't need any instructions on what had to be done. While they were scraping the post, which was as thick as Burnt Hair's muscular thigh and twice the height of a tall man, someone should be readying the hole into which its base would be dropped. Okwaho knelt by that hole. It was not yet ready. It had only been dug down to ankle depth and would have to be at least four times deeper to hold the stockade post in place. A stick that had been shaped from an oak branch into a spoon-shaped digging tool was there on the ground. When any sort of tool was left out that way, Okwaho knew, it was meant for someone to use.

He began to dig, sometimes reversing the digging tool to use its sharpened other end to loosen soil and pry out stones. As he did so, a new song came to him.

Digging, digging
I am digging
Stones rise up
As I am digging

He piled the earth to one side of the hole, the stones to the other. Those rocks, pounded in around the post, would hold it even more firmly.

As always, the song made things easier. He was not

sure how many times he repeated the words, but soon the hole was deep enough. His part of the job was now done. Lifting a post into the hole took at least two grown men.

Okwaho stood and looked around. What else could he do? He walked along the row of posts already in place. When he pushed against them they all held firm—except for one. It moved slightly. It needed earth and stones packed into the ground on the other side.

Okwaho went out and walked along the wall. From the other side he could hear the men working. He located the loose post, placed his digging stick next to it, and went to find stones of the right size. It took some time. He had to walk into the forest till he found a hill with loose stones. When he returned with a heavy armload, he placed the stones on the ground and knelt to begin work. However, just as he was lifting the first stone to pound it into the earth he'd loosened at the base of the post, he heard something. Two men talking softly on the other side of the wall, not aware that he was there. Burnt Hair and his father, Holds the Door Open. Okwaho started to say something. It wasn't right to listen in on other people talking without their knowing.

But then he realized they were talking about Tawis and him.

"There still must be something we can do," Burnt

Hair said. "Were we wrong to decide not to try to plan a raid against them?"

Yes, Okwaho thought. *Yes. Go raid the Oneidas and rescue Tawis!*

"No," Holds the Door Open said, his voice firm. "We moved to this place to escape from war. If we raided, it would have made all our efforts meaningless. Tawis is young and strong. They will not treat him badly, I am sure of that. They were raiding—just as our people have done for more years than can be counted—to get young people to adopt and take the place of others who were killed in warfare. He may be safer among the Oneidas than here in Kanata if Atatarho does send his warriors to attack us. In time, Tawis may become one of them and even forget his life among us."

Those words felt like a knife being stabbed into Okwaho's heart. Could Tawis really forget his old life, forget his best friend? He bit his lip.

"That may all be true," Burnt Hair said. "But what worries me more is how your son is taking this. The two of them were so close, it was as if they had one mind. They were always laughing and doing things together. But now Okwaho walks about as if a dark cloud has come to rest around him. Even if his friend one day no longer remembers his old life, Okwaho will not forget him."

Okwaho put the digging stick down, taking care not to make a sound. He stood up and walked away from those voices that usually gave him comfort but now just deepened his feelings of hopelessness and anger.

chapter eight
CARRIES

Okwaho walked back around the far side of the wall—away from his father and Burnt Hair. Trees and bushes had been cleared away for more than the distance of a long spear throw all around their village. As Okwaho walked, he looked toward the edge of the forest nearest him. At any moment the silence of the forest might be broken by a war cry. Or the swish of an arrow as it came flying through the air toward him.

He finished rounding the stockade wall and walked back through the gate.

Nowhere is safe, he thought.

That thought, too, made him angry.

The little ones, the six other children of their village, were heading toward him, carrying armloads of sticks they'd gathered from close to the stockade. All of them were much younger than Okwaho, and seemed free from care—for now.

With Tawis and Clouds Forming gone, Okwaho was the senior young person in their little village. None of the others were over seven winters old. All of them looked up to Okwaho and sought his guidance.

Before Tawis had been taken, Okwaho had enjoyed such attention. He'd been kind to those children, tried to provide a good model for them just as his elders did for him. He'd even told them stories and sometimes sang songs. But now the anger twisting inside made him impatient. When he spoke to those children, it was never more than a few words.

The biggest of the little ones, Muskrat, came up with an armful of sticks.

"'Kwaho?" Muskrat said, dumping his small armful of sticks on a pile near the central fire. "What should we do now?"

Okwaho stared at him.

What is the matter with you? Are you stupid? That was what he thought of shouting as Muskrat looked up with trusting eyes. It was only with great effort that he held back those hurtful words.

"Gather stones," he said, pointing with his lips in the direction of the corn field. "Birds."

"Nyah wenha, 'Kwaho," Muskrat said. "Thank you. I will do a good job of keeping watch."

A smile on his face, Muskrat turned and ran toward

the corn field, followed by the five other little ones who had held back respectfully when their leader came up to Okwaho, but now were shrieking in delight.

Shooing away birds was their favorite thing to do. It had once been that way for Okwaho back at the big village when he was their age.

Just as had been done at the big village, a small platform had been built in the middle of the corn field. It was a man's height off the ground and just big enough to hold either one grown person or two or three small children sitting in the midst of the several piles of stones that were all just the right size for throwing. When flocks of crows came, looking to pull up the tender new shoots of corn, those stones were used to drive the birds away. That platform also provided a vantage point for whoever was up there to watch for any threat that might be approaching. Doing that work was not just fun, it also made the little ones feel important.

As Okwaho watched them disappear down the hill toward the corn field, he shook his head. It seemed so long ago when he was enjoying life and free of care like that.

I will never be happy again, he thought.

He went back into his family's longhouse and climbed onto his sleeping rack. He felt tired, but was sure he would not sleep.

I will just stay here for a short while. Then I will go try to find something else to do.

Yet when he closed his eyes, the Sleepmaker found him.

He was not sure how long he slept, but when he woke, it was dark outside. He'd slept away the rest of the day. Something had wakened him. What was it? Then he heard it again. A clear, strong voice.

A stranger's voice coming from somewhere outside. And that voice was being answered by the murmur of other voices in response. Okwaho slipped on his moccasins and walked to the door of the longhouse

"That cannot be," a loud voice said. Burnt Hair.

"It is what was said," the stranger's voice replied.

"Then perhaps it is so," a calm, very familiar voice replied. Okwaho's father, Holds the Door Open.

Okwaho pushed the skin door covering aside and looked out. Some people were sitting in a circle around the council fire. Others stood gathered around to listen. It looked as if it was everyone in their village. He knew all of them except for the stranger they were all looking at who sat cross-legged by the fire.

It was hard not to look at him. Not only was he a large, strongly muscled, good-looking man; there were finely drawn blue tattoos on his body. Fish designs decorated each of his cheeks. A bird that looked to be a blue jay spread its wings across his chest. Concentric circles were drawn around his arms and legs.

It was impressive. Many men and women had tattoos, but this man was the first he had ever seen with so many. Such designs were not just meant to look good. They always signified something deeper. If an image came to someone in a dream, it brought power once it was cut into that person's skin.

Having so many tattoos meant that the stranger Okwaho was looking at had much determination and courage. It was a painful process to get a tattoo. First the shape was traced on your body using a piece of charcoal. Then, with either a sharpened bone or a thin-edged piece of flint, the picture would be cut. Painful as it was, that was not the end of it. While the wound was still bleeding, charcoal dust or a special mixture that included the color blue would be put into it. For days after, the one tattooed had to endure not just the pain, but also the constant itching that couldn't be scratched without ruining the design.

Holds the Door Open nodded at Okwaho and then at the ground next to him. Okwaho's mother, Wolf Woman, sitting with the other headwomen across from Holds the Door Open, nodded at her son. Okwaho walked over to sit next to his father.

Okwaho had always felt close to his father. But it was a boy's uncle, the brother of his mother and thus of his own clan, who was supposed to be the most important man in his life. Every father still cared about his own son. Also, Okwaho's father had no sisters who had survived to adulthood. So Holds the Door Open had no nephews. He had also been the lifelong best friend of At the Edge of the Sky, Okwaho's uncle. Their friendship had been as close as that of Okwaho and Tawis, a tie of brotherhood stronger than blood. Until At the Edge of the Sky was killed by enemy raiders, the two of them had shared the duties of teaching Okwaho.

"Tell us again," Holds the Door Open said to the stranger. "Let my son hear your story."

The tattooed man nodded. Then he gently clapped his hands together and spread them out to either side. "It is worth telling often," he said. "So I, Carries, will tell you again. And this time I will tell you more."

The man who had just named himself as Carries did not have the accent of an Onondaga. His accent identified him as a member of the Longhouse Nation closest to the sunrise direction—the Kanienkehaka, the People of the Flint Stone.

Carries leaned forward and smoothed the soft earth around the fire. Then with a long index finger, he drew a rough circle. Then he made a mark below it. "This is the Beautiful Lake and this is our village, four days' walk from here. It began there."

Okwaho listened closely as Carries described what

happened five moons ago. He and three other men of his nation had been fishing by the shore of the lake, which had finally become free of ice with the coming of spring. They were sitting by a fire they'd made, readying their fish traps. Suddenly, one of the men had dropped the fish trap he was holding and picked up his bow and arrows.

"Look!" he shouted. "Look!"

There was something far out on the water to the north. Was it a floating log or a strange water creature? Then they made out what it was. It was a man in a canoe coming from across the lake. They all picked up weapons. Those on the other side of the lake were of the Wendat Nation. Enemies. But as that canoe came closer, the man with the bow and arrows lowered his weapon because what they saw was so strange. That canoe looked to be made of white, glistening stone. The man in it was not holding a shield or dressed in the armor made of slats of wood fastened together that the Wendats sometimes wore into battle. All he had on was clothing made of white buckskin—almost the same color as his canoe. His arms were spread wide open, showing he held no weapons. And though he was not paddling, the wind blowing at his back was pushing him and his canoe that seemed made of marble toward the four men on the shore.

Carries laughed. "It was only when he got much closer that we saw his canoe—even though it was not like our dugouts—was not made of stone. It was pure white because it was made of birch bark. But, still, the way he came toward us, arms open, chest exposed, surprised us. You know how it is these days. The first thing when you see a stranger is to guess that he is an enemy. The second thing is to kill him before he can try to kill you."

Carries turned to look at Burnt Hair and Holds the Door Open. "Again, I must thank you for allowing me into your village and not killing me when you saw me. I had heard your little village was one opposed to fighting. That is why I came here first."

"Huh," Burnt Hair snorted. "We can always kill you later."

"He is joking," Holds the Door Open said.

"A little," Burnt Hair said, making a serious face. Then everyone laughed. Teasing was always a good thing—a way to lighten the atmosphere and sometimes remind someone they were not more important than anyone else.

Holds the Door Open reached into the fire and pulled out one of the ears of corn that had been roasting there. He handed it to Carries. "Here," he said. "Sharing food with you proves that you are welcome here as a guest."

"Or that we want to fatten you up before we eat you," Burnt Hair added.

Carries held up the ear of corn, its husk blackened from the hot coals. "I thank this corn for giving its gift of life to us all."

The other men nodded at his words. Giving thanks was always the right way. He peeled back the husk, picked free a few kernels and ate them. Then he placed the ear of corn in his lap.

"I will say more about how that man I have described came to us," he said.

He spoke then of how that canoe had beached itself into the sand. How that man, a tall straight-standing person with a gentle smile on his face, had stepped out of it.

"I am Skennerahowi, the Peacemaker," the tall stranger then told them. *"I have come with a message from our Creator. The message I bring is that of peace."*

"We could understand his words," Carries said. "Even though he was Wendat and spoke our language with a strange accent. There was something about him that made him seem different from other men. You could feel the presence of orenda, spiritual power, flowing from him. It was like a wave that washed over us. It touched something inside each of us. We listened as he continued to speak, telling us about his birth."

chapter nine

THE BIRTH OF SKENNERAHOWI

The Peacemaker's mother lived with her grandmother in a small lodge removed from their main village on the other side of the Beautiful Lake from the lands of the Longhouse Nations. Even there, though, there was no such thing as peace. All around them, the women and children and elders lived in constant fear. Any moment the terrible war cry might be heard and enemies would sweep into the village, killing people and taking captives.

Because the men of that village thought of nothing but war and revenge, and her granddaughter's parents were dead, the grandmother decided to move them to a new place, a hidden cove by the side of the lake, a place where no one else ever went. The two of them lived alone there, safe from the danger of enemy raids.

The grandmother kept a close eye on her grand-daughter. Even though she had come of child-bearing age, she was not yet married. However, it became obvious that she was expecting a child.

Tell me who the father is, her grandmother asked.

I do not know, her granddaughter replied. *I have never been with a man.*

The grandmother refused to believe her granddaughter. She kept asking and asking, but the answer was always the same.

I do not know. I have never been with a man.

Why was her beloved granddaughter lying? Perhaps, she thought, some evil spirit had done this at night while the innocent girl was sleeping. Yes, that must be it.

So when her granddaughter's child was born—a handsome, smiling boy—the grandmother decided that the boy had to be evil. He would only bring them bad luck.

I must get rid of this child, the grandmother decided. *There is no other way.*

She waited until her daughter was sleeping, took down a stone ax from the place where it hung on the wall, and stuck it under her belt. As she lifted the child, the boy smiled up at her with great warmth and reached out one small hand to gently caress her cheek. For a moment, that smile touched her heart. But she shook her head. She knew what must be done.

She walked outside. A cold wind was blowing from the direction of the winter land. The ice on the big lake was frozen solid.

Taking a long pole from the firewood stacked outside, she began to walk out onto the lake, leaning into the wind. She walked until, when she looked back, their little longhouse seemed no bigger than a brown fallen leaf. Then she chopped a hole in the thick ice. When she was done she lifted up her great-grandson and quickly dropped him into the freezing water. Picking up the long pole, she used it to shove the baby far under the ice. Then she shoved ice and snow into the hole until there was no sign it had ever been there.

Without looking over her shoulder, she trudged back to the lodge. But even before she pushed aside the heavy skin hung over the door, she heard the sound from inside of an infant cooing. When she looked inside, what she saw made her knees weak. Her granddaughter was sitting by the fire and held in her arms, smiling and making little happy sounds, was that boy.

Now the grandmother was sure that the child was evil. How else could any being, especially a tiny baby, have survived the icy water of the big lake? And how could it have appeared back in the lodge before she returned? So she did not give up on her plan to get rid of him.

The next day, she walked deep into the forest. Under a great pine tree, she cleared away the deep snow from a patch of ground. The earth was frozen on top, but she worked hard to break through the icy soil with that stone ax. Then she began to dig. When the hole was as deep as her waist, she climbed out and went back to the lodge where her granddaughter had just finished feeding the baby.

"Here," the grandmother said, holding out her arms. "Let me take him outside. The fresh air will do him good."

"I am sure that is so," her granddaughter said, handing the baby to her grandmother without hesitation.

The grandmother went outside. As she carried the boy toward the hole she'd dug, he reached up both hands to touch her chin and looked up into her eyes.

"No," the grandmother said. "No."

She dropped the child into the hole and began to shove the earth over him. When the hole was filled and she had stomped the soil down hard, she pushed a great mound of snow over it, leaving no trace of what she had done.

"The earth will surely hold him," she said, wiping off her hands.

But when she went back into the lodge, the first thing she saw was that evil child, once again cooing in his mother's arms.

That night the grandmother did not sleep. What could she do now? Clearly the baby's evil magic was strong. But she could not give up. There had to be a way. Then it came to her. There was an answer. Evil could not survive against the cleansing flames of fire.

The next day she made a fire some distance from their lodge. She piled on dry branches and then logs. Before long it was burning so hot, she had to step back from it.

She went back into the lodge, her forehead beaded with sweat from the fire's heat.

"Give me the baby," she said.

Without a word, her face calm, her granddaughter did as her grandmother asked.

As the grandmother carried the infant, he kept smiling up at her. The boy was still smiling as she lifted him and hurled him into the heart of the raging fire. Then she piled on even more wood. She stayed there watching until the fire had burned itself out and there was nothing left but ashes.

"Now," she said, "now his evil is certainly gone from the world."

But when she returned to their lodge, just as had happened each time before, she heard the happy sound of the infant's laughter before she even pulled back the skin door.

That night, once again she could not sleep. She sat on her sleeping rack, unsure what to do next. Then, in the midst of the night, she heard someone scratch on the door of the lodge. She looked up and saw the shadowy shape of a tall man standing before her.

A man's deep voice spoke, a voice that she heard more in her heart than in her ears.

"I have come from the west," the shadowy shape said. "I bring you a message. Your granddaughter has done nothing wrong. She has told you the truth. Her son is good. He was sent by the Creator to bring peace. There is too much blood being shed among the people of the earth. When he has grown to manhood, he will travel among the different nations and bring them the message of peace. He will be known as Skennerahowi, the Peacemaker. Now you must stop trying to harm your great-grandson."

Then that shadowy figure walked away and disappeared into the darkness.

The next day, when the grandmother looked outside she saw in the new snow the tracks of a giant hare leading away from the door of their lodge toward the direction of the sunset. She knew then that she had been visited by a messenger from the Creator. From that day on she showed nothing but love toward her blessed great-grandson.

chapter ten
THE COHOES FALLS

When Carries was done with his tale, everyone was silent for a while.

Then Burnt Hair spoke. "That is an interesting story," he said.

A wonderful story! Okwaho thought. It was a story that made him feel something deep inside himself, something other than anger. What was it? Hope. That was it. That was what he felt, for the first time in a long time, hope like a small bird just beginning to flutter its wings.

"It is a good story," Carries agreed.

"But you did not see it," Holds the Door Open said in a neutral voice.

"No," Carries replied. "But I saw him. I heard his voice. It is true that I can only tell you the story as he told it to us. But it is also true that I felt the power of his message as I listened to those words. I felt the truth of it. I can tell you that I felt as if the man who told that story was not trying to deceive us. He truly was Skennerahowi, the one who would bring peace to all of us."

"I see," Burnt Hair said.

Burnt Hair was not an easy man to impress. But Okwaho could hear a note of awe in his voice. He had felt moved beyond words when Carries spoke the Peacemaker's story. He looked around at the gathered people and saw they were feeling what he was feeling.

"His words changed you," Holds the Door Open said to Carries.

Carries nodded. "I had another name then, but I threw it away on the day I heard his words of peace. I became one who would help carry that message. I became Carries."

He placed his hand on the bird tattooed on his chest. "I had this cut into my skin, as a sign that I would be a message carrier for the rest of my days."

Of course, Okwaho thought. *Of all the birds, it is always blue jay who first calls out to alert all to danger approaching.*

Carries looked down at his hands as if they were holding something—even though they looked to be empty.

"That is not the only story you have to tell us, is it?" Okwaho's mother, Wolf Woman, said.

Everyone turned to look at her. Although Atatarho

no longer listened to the wise words of women, words that had always guided all the Longhouse Nations in the past, everyone in their small breakaway village not only remembered that time but always honored the words of their women. In fact, it was the women who headed each of their families who made the final decision to leave the big village among the hills.

"No," the tattooed man said. "I have another story to tell about the Peacemaker if you want to hear it."

"We do," Wolf Woman replied.

Carries reached into the larger of the two pouches that hung at his belt. The shape of a tree in red dyed porcupine quills had been sewn onto it with sinew. He opened his pouch, reached in, and took from it a stone. He touched the stone to his chest and then his lips before holding it up for everyone to see.

"This stone is one I took from the River of Rapids, from the place called Cohoes where there is a great waterfall. It is not far from the River Beyond the Openings, Skanehtateh Kahuntah. Our Flint Stone People tell an old story about that waterfall. They say that long ago a great monster was defeated there, thrown over that waterfall to its death. It was a beast as big as a hill, covered with long hair. It had two great teeth that stuck out like spears and a long lip that it could use to grab people. Have you heard of that creature?"

People nodded, Okwaho among them. His mother

had told him about that beast, the Walking Hill. It lived long ago and attacked villages, crushing people under its feet. Finally the Holder Up of the Heavens came to earth and destroyed it.

Carries smiled. "I am not going to say more about that. I only mention it so that you may have in your mind the image of the place where something great happened. I am going to tell you the story of the Peacemaker at Cohoes Falls."

One morning, the people of the Flint Stone village near the great waterfalls woke as they always did to greet the first light of the sun and give thanks for the new day. That was when they saw a thin feather of smoke rising from the direction of the falls. They knew it meant that someone was announcing his presence and asking through that smoke permission to enter their village.

Their great war chief, a man of the Turtle Clan—for theirs was a Turtle Clan village—called two runners to him.

"Go," he said, "see who has sent up that smoke and if that person has come in peace. If not, then kill him."

Those two men did as their chief asked. When they arrived at the hill overlooking the falls where a single tall tree hung out over the rushing water, they found a stranger sitting and smoking his pipe.

"Come here," that stranger said in a calm voice. "I mean you no harm. I have something to tell you."

The two runners approached the man warily. He seemed to have no weapons, but in this time when war and fighting were everywhere, they knew they had to be careful.

"What do you want?" the first runner asked.

"I want to enter your village," the man who was the Peacemaker said. "I have an important message for your war chief and all your people."

"Hah," the second runner said. "Who are you? Why should we not just kill you right here?"

"I am Skennerahowi," the Peacemaker replied. "Before you kill me, I ask you to tell your war chief I wish to talk with him. If he does not agree, then you can come back and kill me."

The two runners looked at each other. No one had ever spoken to them that way before, showing neither anger nor fear.

"We will take that message to our war chief," the first runner said.

"Thank you," the Peacemaker said. "I will wait here for your return."

When they got back to the village, the two runners

told the great war chief about the calm man they had found sitting on the hill overlooking the falls.

"I have heard of this one from my assistant chiefs. I doubted what he told me. But now I would like to see this brave man," the war chief said. "Bring him back to our village."

When the Peacemaker arrived at the village, he found that a place had been made for him to sit in front of the war chief and his two assistants. As soon as the Peacemaker had been seated, the war chief stood up and spoke to all the people gathered around them.

"I think I know who this man is," he said. "I believe this is the one we heard about who arrived from across the lake bringing a great message. My second war chief has spoken about this man, saying that his message about peace sounded good to him. I could not believe that what he said was true, but now this man has shown up here. So let us listen to him now."

When the war chief finished speaking, he sat down and the Peacemaker stood up.

"It is true," he said. "I sent a message with the first men I met, men of the Flint Stone Nation. I asked them to spread the word that I was coming to bring a better way of living than warfare to the People of the Longhouse. It is a way that begins with peace. When our minds are good and we all are of one mind, then peace may begin. Our Creator is sad that our people are killing each other.

So many good people have died. I have come to stop the fighting and bring back the peace we were meant to live in. Long ago, our Creator placed us here to live in harmony with each other, to always show kindness and respect each other. But your minds have been twisted by war. What you must do now is give up those weapons of war. New leaders who will always be men of peace must be raised up by the clan mothers. And those men can only remain as leaders as long as they do not go to war. If they do not do their duty, they must give their title back to the clan mothers. The job of those new leaders will always be to keep the peace strong."

When the Peacemaker sat down, the second war chief was pleased. Perhaps, he thought, the people will now listen to this message and peace will actually come.

But then the great war chief stood up again. "I like this message. However, I am not sure that it is possible. I doubt that it will work."

The war chief then sat down and his first assistant stood up. He had made fun in recent days of the second assistant war chief for believing such an impossible thing as one man being able to bring an end to all warfare between the different nations.

"I agree with our great leader," the first assistant war chief said. "I do not trust this stranger." He looked over at the second assistant war chief and shook his head. "I think he must prove himself. If he is truly a messenger from the Creator, then he must have the Creator's protection. Let us test him. Does everyone agree?"

He looked around the circle of people gathered. No one spoke against his idea. Then he looked hard at the Peacemaker. "Do you agree to whatever test we choose for you?"

"I agree as long as all the people are there to see what happens."

"Good," the chief's first assistant said. "This is how you will be tested. At the edge of the cliff over the great waterfall there is a big tree. One of its branches reaches out over the falls. Tomorrow we will all go to that tree. You must climb out and sit on that branch and stay there as our warriors cut the branch from the tree. All the people will watch as you fall to your death."

"I will do as you ask," the Peacemaker said, his voice as calm as ever.

When the sun rose the next day, everyone gathered at the gorge. They watched as the chief and his two assistants and a small group of warriors carrying stone hatchets led the calm stranger to that tree above the rushing water. They continued to watch as the doomed man climbed out to the end of that branch. Using their sharp stone hatchets, the warriors chopped at that branch until it broke off the tree. They still watched as the Peacemaker was swept over the falls and was lost from sight in the foamy water striking the jagged rocks far, far below. They kept watching, but although the branch bobbed up and was carried down the river by the swift current, there was no sign of that foolhardy man who had claimed to be the Creator's messenger.

Everyone returned to the village and gathered around the war chief.

"You have all seen what happened," he said. "That man was brave, but now he is gone."

Everyone agreed, even the second assistant war chief, whose heart was filled with sadness. Although everyone else slept soundly that night, that one man stayed awake, praying to the Creator.

Before daybreak woke the village, he was the first to leave his lodge. He looked toward the direction of the great waterfalls and in the early light before dawn saw a plume of smoke lifting like a raised hand. When he told the great war chief what he had seen, the chief sent two runners to see who was now camping by the river.

As soon as they came in sight of the little hill above the falls, they saw who was there. Sitting in front of his fire and smoking a pipe was the man who had gone over the falls when they cut the branch he'd been sitting upon. Seeing him frightened them. After what they had done, would this man who clearly had great power seek to do them harm?

"Who are you?" the first of the runners asked him.

"I am Skennerahowi. I am the one you saw fall into the gorge," he said. "Do you need more proof that I have come to bring peace?"

"We believe you," the men replied. "Come back to our village."

"Go back and tell your chief to make ready. I will come there soon. But I will not stay long, for I have much more work to do and many more to visit."

The runners went back to their village and told the great war chief what they had seen.

"We will prepare a special place for him," the chief said, and he gathered everyone in the village. When the Peacemaker arrived, they made two lines of people for him to walk between on his way to the council house. There he was welcomed and given a seat of honor by the chief's side.

"We asked you for proof," the great war chief said. "You have given us that proof. I had been waiting for your arrival, hoping that peace might be possible. Now I believe it to be so. I accept your message."

Then the two assistant war chiefs spoke. "We accept your message as well."

"Do all of the people accept the message of the Peacemaker?" the head war chief asked.

And all of the people answered with one voice, "Yes."

The Peacemaker stood then and looked around at everyone gathered there, waiting to hear his words.

"Now," he said, "we will soon enter a new time, a time of peace. We will all have a good mind, speak with one voice, and live together as one family. No longer will we have chiefs who lead us to war. Now we will elevate new kinds of leaders, men of good mind who will be known as royaners, peace chiefs."

He turned to the head war chief. "You, great leader of the Flint Stone Nation, your name will always be spoken first in the roll call of these new chiefs because you were awaiting my arrival. Even though you doubted me, you came to accept this message. So your name will be He Who Was of Two Minds. I appoint the women of your clan to watch over you and make sure you always keep a good mind and abide by the will of the council of the clan mothers. When you leave this world, they are the ones who will choose whoever follows you and carries that same name."

The Peacemaker then turned to the second assistant war chief, the one who had never doubted him.

"You, great leader, you never slept while awaiting my arrival. You spoke about my message of peace before anyone else. Now you will put away all thoughts of fighting and war. You will do the work of our Creator and you will find a way to remember all that happens here. You will be second on the roll call of the royaners, but first among them. Your name will be Hiawatha, He Who Is Awake. Soon, but not yet, you will travel by my side and become my voice."

Then the Peacemaker turned to the first assistant war chief. "You doubted me and you were confused about what to do. But you also came to accept the message of peace. So you, too, will no longer be a war chief. Instead, you will work on behalf of the people. Because your decision would have gone either way, your name will be Equal Height. Like your two brother peace chiefs and all others who become royaners, the women of your clan will advise you and raise up whoever follows you to carry that name and responsibility when you leave this world."

He Who Was of Two Minds spoke then. "It is good that we will follow the way of peace. But what of those who have not accepted this peace? How will be defend ourselves if they attack us?"

"I am going now to speak to those other nations, to bring them the message of peace. When all of you People of the Longhouse are of one mind, no longer will you fight with each other. You will use your good minds to avoid conflict and come to agreement together. Because your nations joined together will be strong, that strength will prevent other nations from attacking you. But even with other nations, you must use persuasion and the power of the good mind to prevent war."

The Peacemaker looked around again at the people who were listening closely to his every word.

"I am going now to visit other nations and bring them this message of peace. There will come a time when all of us will be called to gather at Onondaga, where a giant war chief controls others with his power. But first I must clear a path."

Then the Peacemaker, his face turned toward the direction of the sunset, left them.

When Carries had finished his second story about the Peacemaker, everyone was silent. It was not just that Carries was such a good storyteller, his voice even and calm, each word clearly spoken. It was the story itself that brought such thoughtful silence.

Especially to Okwaho. That story was magic.

It had not been like listening. It had been as if he had been carried there, placed to stand at the edge of the cliff and see it happen, watching the Peacemaker plunge into the great waterfall and then—with those men who saw his smoke rising the next day—feel the same wonder they must have felt at his miraculous survival.

Okwaho looked around at his father, his mother,

Burnt Hair and all the others who had been listening as intently as he. The looks on their faces were the same. Even Burnt Hair was nodding his head.

Finally Wolf Woman broke the silence.

"Will we see this man?" she asked. "Will he come here?"

Carries smiled. "Yes. And it will be soon, before Grandmother Moon's face is full again in the sky. Those of us who have been carrying the message that he will soon arrive have now visited almost every village. The Great Stone People, the Swampy Land People and my own Flint nation have all come to the decision to join their minds and heart together. I have just come from the village of the Standing Stone People closest to yours and they, too, have said they are willing to give up the way of war—as long as the Onondagas agree to the Great Peace. It seems that your great war chief, Atatarho, will be the last one to decide."

chapter eleven
THE BLUEBIRD

Okwaho sat in his sleeping rack, thinking of what had happened.

"Da neho," Carries had said. "That is all I have to say. I am done." Then he had looked around at the people of their little village.

"What does everyone think?" Wolf Woman had asked.

And there had been no hesitation on the part of anyone in their little village. Everyone had agreed they should welcome the Peacemaker when he came at last to them. A desire for peace was the reason they had left Onondaga.

Okwaho thought of the look on the face of Carries as he told them about the Peacemaker. It was a look of calm, of belief. Of hope. A similar expression had come to the faces of his mother and father as they heard the Peacemaker's message. His father had been so convinced that he had agreed to travel with Carries to other villages, helping them prepare for the coming of the man himself.

Okwaho lay back on his sleeping rack. But as soon as he closed his eyes, he began to think of something else. Those he'd lost. Peace could not bring them back. And with that thought the anger that had briefly left his mind came flowing back in like a black river.

Even if a new dawn of peace did come, it would be too late for those who had been killed or taken away as captives. His uncle, At the Edge of the Sky, would still be dead. His best friend would remain far away, being taught to forget his old life, his former friends, even his name.

All of Okwaho's excitement faded away as those dark depressing thoughts, like clouds bringing cold rain, settled around his shoulders.

When the Sleepmaker finally came, sleep brought him little rest. Instead, it dropped him into a dream. He found himself reliving the events of that day when his friend was caught. He woke up again and again during the night, sitting up and shouting "No!" It was not until just before dawn when he finally fell into an exhausted and dreamless sleep.

Okwaho looked up at the elm bark roof of their longhouse and sighed. His stomach felt as if a fist were clenched inside it. He swung his legs over the side and dropped down to the floor. A pot full of chestnut mush hung over the fire, left there by his mother so he would have food when he woke. But he did not want to eat. He did not know what he wanted. He pushed open the skin door and went outside. He walked past the men working on the wall.

Muskrat and the five other little children came running up to him.

"'Kwaho, what shall we do today?" Muskrat asked.

Okwaho paid no attention to him. He just kept walking until he passed through the open gate of the stockade.

Okwaho was not sure where he was going as he walked. But even though he felt as if a wrestling match were going on inside his head, he stayed alert. He would not go far from the walls of their settlement. He would not be foolish as he and Tawis had been. He would stay where he could see—and be seen from—their village. He just needed enough space to be by himself.

Finally, his feet led him to the top of the small hill just a bit farther than an arrow's flight from their stockade's walls. He could easily see their community, the nearby river where the women of their village were already working in the corn field they'd planted where the spring flood had deposited fertile soil. Their stockade sat in the middle of a wide clearing. Removing all the brush and trees around their new home and their fields had been one of the first things they had done as soon as the decision to move had been made. That way—during the daytime at least—no one would be able to approach without being seen. At night fires were kept burning and sentinels were always posted. Even though their desire was to live in peace, it did not mean they would hesitate to defend themselves and their families.

The moss was thick and dry near the base of a chestnut tree. He and Tawis had come here often. It was a good place to sit—especially since the two boys had carefully cleared away all of the thorny chestnut burrs that encased the sweet-tasting nuts that fell here in abundance each autumn.

As he sat there, a bluebird came and rested on the low-hanging branch of the nearest chestnut tree. It bobbed its head at him, then began its low-pitched warbling song, repeating it again and again. It was as if the bird were trying to send him a message. His mother often told him to listen closely to everything around him. Sometimes a bird call or the sound of the wind in the trees might be telling you something that you need to know, she said. If you listen long enough and well enough, you can sometimes understand what the natural world around you is trying to say. It might be advice or perhaps a warning. You may even become one of those people, a real listener, one who understands almost everything the forest is saying.

Okwaho listened hard to the bluebird's song. It was pleasant to hear, but was it more than that? Was the little bird telling him not to give up hope? Or was it just singing to tell the world this branch, this tree belonged to it? He was trying to become a good listener, but what was he hearing?

Okwaho shook his head. He could not understand anything. Not only the bluebird's song, but why his friend had been taken, why so many loved war. Why so many others seemed to accept that things could not be changed, that to hope for peace was a foolish wish.

Someone cleared his throat behind him. His leg muscles tensed. He almost jumped up to run. But just as quickly he realized that whoever it was behind him was trying not to startle him. That was why he—and it was surely a man from the deepness of his voice—had politely announced his presence. Plus, that bluebird was still singing on the branch. Perhaps it was telling him there was nothing to fear from whoever just arrived.

"Gwey-gwey," the man said in a soft voice. "Hello."

Okwaho turned. It was Carries, the one who had arrived with the message about the Peacemaker.

"I hope I did not startle you," the tattooed man said. He smiled as he said those words. That small, gently teasing smile showed he knew he had almost made Okwaho jump out of his skin. "I have always had this habit of walking quietly. It is even more necessary these days as I go from village to village. Even though I carry a message of peace, I'm still traveling through a land of war."

The way Carries spoke to him was good to hear. The man's voice was soft but confident, and the light in his eyes showed he believed in what he was doing.

"Gwey-gwey," Okwaho replied, though he did not smile back in return. The last time a smile had come to him had been that day when he and Tawis were fishing. Perhaps he would never smile again.

"This is a pleasant place. May I join you?" Carries looked up at the bluebird, still bobbing and trilling its song. "You and your small friend there?"

Okwaho reached out and touched the mossy ground next to him.

Carries sat down. He did not speak for a time. Neither did Okwaho. The two of them listened to the bluebird. Every now and then Carries would nod his head—as if understanding what the bird was saying. Perhaps he was one of those people his mother had told him about, a real listener.

Finally the bird finished its song, then bobbed its head up and down, as if saying farewell. Then it fluttered away.

Carries cleared his throat again. "You are Okwaho," he said.

Okwaho looked at him.

"I have heard from your mother about what happened," Carries said. "A hard thing."

Okwaho drew in a breath, then bit his lip. What right did a stranger have to talk with him about this? Part of his mind wanted to tell him to go away and leave him alone. But another part of his mind was thinking differently. *Let this man speak,* it was telling him. Carries had told such good stories, perhaps he would tell another one now. Okwaho put his hand to his forehead, trying to sort out the confusion he was feeling.

"It is a very hard thing to lose a friend," Carries said. "I had a twin brother. His name was He Is Standing. He was taken by war. But he was not taken as a captive like your friend. An enemy arrow pierced his heart. I held him in my arms and felt his spirit leave. I felt broken. My mind became so full of loss and anger that all I could think about was revenge. I needed to take one of their lives in return."

Okwaho looked at Carries. The man's voice had grown deeper as he spoke of that loss.

"Did you do that?" Okwaho asked. "Take revenge?"

"Oh yes," Carries said. He patted his right arm and then held up both hands as if aiming a bow and releasing an arrow. "I was a good warrior then." He slapped his hands together. "I took one of their lives." He slapped his hands a second time. "And then I killed another."

Carries shook his head. "But it did no good. The pain I felt in my mind did not go away. Not until I met . . . him."

Carries took a deep breath and looked off into the distance. It was as if he was going back to that moment of meeting the Peacemaker. Okwaho said nothing, waiting until the man was ready to speak again, but also eager now to hear what he would say. Perhaps it actually would lift his heart and give him hope.

chapter twelve
A FIRE THAT IS BURNING

Carries nodded his head as if he'd just heard something spoken that only he could hear. Whatever it was, it brought a small smile to his lips, making the tattooed fish twitch its tail. He turned back to Okwaho.

"Do you know how someone looks when they are bringing good news? Like a grandmother announcing to the people the birth of her first grandchild? Or perhaps a hunter returning from the forest carrying a deer over his shoulders? Imagine such a look on someone's face and then imagine that look being many times as happy and self-assured. That is the way the face of the stranger in white appeared to us. So, even before he spoke before our council, I was ready to listen.

"His words to the council were simple and clear, as clear as water that seems shallow but is actually very deep. He told us he had come as a messenger from the Creator, who was not pleased to see the human beings always fighting each other and suffering. He said he had come to help bring us together as we were meant to be."

Then Carries coughed out a laugh. "Do you remember the story I told? How we were by the lake and saw him approaching in that strange white canoe?"

Okwaho nodded.

"I was not the first to reach him. Long Feather, our fast runner, got there a spear's throw ahead of me.

"'*Throw down your weapons,*' Long Feather shouted, drawing his bow and aiming an arrow at the tall, good-looking man's chest.

"But that tall man, simply stepped from his canoe and held out his empty hands. '*I carry no weapons,*' he said.

"Long Feather stopped and lowered his bow. The stranger's voice had been so calm that it confused him.

"By then I was at Long Feather's side. I held in my hands the rawhide cords I always carried on my belt. They were there to bind the hands of any strangers we encountered so that we could bring them back to our village as a prisoner. The other two men with me, Caller and Beaver Tail, had picked up their war clubs.

"The man gestured at us. '*You do not need those,*' he said. '*I have come to speak to you all. Bring me to your council. First, though, let me put out your fire. A fire that is left burning and not properly put out is like anger or revenge. It may end up destroying everything.*'

"His words were so strange and yet rang so true that none of the four of us questioned him. We did not bind his hands or threaten him. We just stood there like children waiting for a parent to tell us what to do.

"As we watched, he carefully put out that small fire, first pouring water on it and then covering it with the loose earth he had placed around it. When he was done, there was no sign that a fire had ever been there.

"Then, walking ahead of us as if the path to our village had been made especially for his feet to walk it, he led the way. Everyone was waiting. None of us had run ahead to tell them to gather as they did, yet they were all there waiting. Even our dogs did not bark at him as he entered our stockade. Bear Killer, the strongest of our dogs, the one that was the leader of all the other dogs, came up to him and licked his hand.

"Smiling and nodding at our children, the stranger went straight to our council house where our elders were waiting. Then, as we all listened, he spoke of his strange birth and of the Great Peace that he was bringing."

Again, Carries stopped and lifted his head as if listening.

"It happened that way?" Okwaho said. "Everyone accepted his words?"

Carries cupped his chin in his hand. "No," he said. "Not everyone was ready at first to hear his message. Holds the Rattle, one of our elders, asked him why we should make peace. Our young men were strong warriors. If anyone dared to attack us and killed one of our people, we would quickly take revenge and kill one of their people in return."

Okwaho nodded. He had heard that sort of thing said before . . . especially by Atatarho, the Entangled One, the black snakes in his hair hissing as he spoke.

"How did the Peacemaker answer Holds the Rattle?" Okwaho asked.

"First," Carries said, "he looked around at us, at our confident young men, our leaders who seemed so sure of themselves.

"Then the Peacemaker nodded his head. *'I agree,'* he told us. *'I can see that your young men are strong. I have no doubt the warriors of your village will fight well against any who might dare attack you. But is that not also true of other villages? Is it not true that they also have strong warriors and determined leaders? Can any man, no matter how strong, survive when an arrow pierces his heart? Have any of your young men died in battle?'*

"Only a season ago we had lost three men in battle against other Mohawks—men of our own nation from another community a day's walk from ours—the Village by the Rapids. So the man's words struck home. Even Holds the Rattle had to nod his head. But the Peacemaker was not done speaking.

"*'Let me tell you a story,'* he said."

Carries looked at Okwaho. "Would you like to hear it?"

"Yes."

"Good. This is the story he told, the story of the Great Battle."

Long ago, there was a boy named Rabbit Foot. He had a special gift. He was able to understand the languages of animals and speak back to them as if they were human beings. One day he was out walking through the forest when he heard a sound. Somewhere a great battle was being fought. He followed that sound until he came to a hill. When he climbed that hill and looked down to the other side he saw the ones who were fighting. There, in a clearing in the woods, a giant snake was struggling with a huge frog. The snake had caught the frog by its hind legs and was starting to swallow it as the frog tried to pull itself free.

Rabbit Foot walked down to take a closer look.

"My friend," he said to the frog, "your enemy really has you."

"That is true," the huge frog croaked, still trying to escape. "That is true. Can you help me? Can you help me?"

Rabbit Foot had been taught by his elders not to inter-fere with the natural course of things. It was natural for one animal to eat another. So he did not try to free the frog from the snake's jaws.

But he did notice that the snake was lying on the ground in something very close to a circle. Its tail was right in front of the big frog's mouth. Offering advice would not really be interfering, would it?

"My friend," Rabbit Foot said to the frog. "Perhaps you could do to your enemy what your enemy is doing to you?"

"Good idea, good idea," the frog said. It reached out with its front legs and grabbed the snake's tail and stuffed it into its mouth. Then it began to swallow.

As the frog swallowed and the snake continued swallowing, that circle they formed got smaller and smaller.

This is getting interesting, Rabbit Foot thought.

The snake swallowed and the frog swallowed, the snake swallowed and the frog swallowed. And the circle got smaller and smaller until . . .

The Peacemaker clapped his hands together. "Pop!" he said. "They both disappeared. They had eaten each other."

Carries smiled so broadly that it seemed as if the fish tattoo was going to swim off his face. "At first, some of us laughed. Others shook their heads. It was the sort of funny story that you might tell to a child. But then the story's deeper meaning began to sink in. Like all of our stories, what the Peacemaker had related to us was meant to entertain and teach. Whether we were the frog or the snake, always fighting with each other would end up in both being wiped out. From that point on, everyone in our village began to listen to what the Peacemaker was saying. And in the end, it was agreed by all of us. We would join in his plan to bring the Great Peace."

Okwaho looked down at their small walled village. The Peacemaker's story made sense to him. Like so many stories that seemed simple at first, it contained a lesson. It was a lesson that could be applied in more ways than one. It was about the results of war—but it was also about him. He had been holding on to his anger for so long—like that snake holding on to the frog. If he did not let go, that anger would eat him. He would either be destroyed or become as twisted as Atatarho. It had cleared some of the clouds from around his head. He saw now that there was a way forward. It was a way as simple and clear as that story of the boy Rabbit Foot. It was a way that required him to let go of his anger, to clear the clouds from around his head. To no longer look back and regret the past, but to look forward. He turned to Carries.

"I want to follow the Peacemaker's way," he said. "What can I do?"

chapter thirteen
KEEP LISTENING

Carries placed his hand on Okwaho's shoulder. "What can you do, my young friend?" he asked. "Do what you are doing now. Keep listening. And be ready."

He stood and brushed himself off. "I have delivered my message here. Now I must move on to other villages and tell them to prepare. The Peacemaker will soon come."

"Soon?" Okwaho said, rising to his own feet.

Carries nodded. "He has been to almost every other place in our land where the people have been suffering from endless war. But the last place he will come, I have been told, is Onondaga, to the big village your people left. That is where everyone, people from all of our Longhouse Nations, will gather to bring the Great Peace into being."

"But what about Atatarho?" Okwaho asked, seeing in his mind the angry face of their powerful, giant leader who had sworn that none were greater than him.

"The Peacemaker will speak to him," Carries said. "And the Peacemaker will not come alone. He will have many people of our different nations behind him. And by his side will be his two greatest allies. Tsakonsaseh, the Mother of Nations, is the first of them."

"Tsakonsase?" Okwaho said. Hers was a name he had heard before. Of course he had heard her name. Everyone knew her name. Her neutral lodge was far to the west where the war trails crossed. Anyone seeking shelter could come to her lodge and she would welcome them. She was known for giving advice to any warrior who sought her help. It was said that the path to war led through her lodge of peace. "Is that the same Tsakonsaseh whose lodge is by the huge waterfall?"

"Yes," Carries said. "But she has left that lodge. The Peacemaker visited her and told her that a new day was coming. No longer, he told her, would she advise men about war. Instead she would help them remain firm to the practice of peace. It is said that she was the first to say she would follow this new path and help him bring the Great Peace. And because of that, it would be she and the women of the clans who would choose all our leaders in the future. So, from that time when she joined forces with the Peacemaker, she also began to carry the name of Mother of Nations. When the Peacemaker arrives at Onondaga, she will be with him."

Okwaho took a deep breath. Tsakonsaseh would be

coming to Onondaga, by the Peacemaker's side? It was almost too much to believe. It was as if he had stepped from everyday life into the middle of a great story. But Carries had said that there would be two by the Peacemaker's side.

"Who is the second one who will be with him?"

"Ah," Carries said, the smile on his face growing broader. "It is one whose name you've already heard. Hiawatha. Do you remember?"

Okwaho remembered. Hiawatha was in the story Carries had told about the Peacemaker's arrival. Hiawatha was the second assistant war chief of the people of the Flint Stone Village near Cohoes Falls, the first to believe the Peacemaker's message. The new name of Hiawatha, He Who Is Awake, had been given him by the Peacemaker. He was to be the first among those new peace chiefs. What were they to be called? Royaners?

Okwaho nodded.

Carries smiled. "There is more to tell about him," he said, "what happened to him after the Peacemaker left their village. This is the story of Hiawatha's great loss."

Of all the people of the Flint Stone, no one was a better speaker than Hiawatha. Everyone listened to his deep sonorous voice when he stood up in council to offer his opinion. He always seemed to think first of others and try to help them. Hiawatha was liked by everyone. He was a good father and had three daughters he loved dearly. Their mother had walked on from this life when the girls were young, but Hiawatha had taken good care of them. And now that the promise of peace had been brought to the people, he thought their futures would be bright and untroubled by war.

One by one, Hiawatha's daughters became sick. No medicine was able to cure them and one by one they died. The loss of his daughters filled Hiawatha with such grief that he could no longer live among the people. His mind became clouded. He left the Flint Stone People and disappeared into the forest. Many had gone searching for Hiawatha, hoping to bring him back. But Hiawatha had been as elusive as a panther and all they had been able to find were the remains of cold campfires.

What had caused the death of his daughters? It was the work of Atatarho. Word of the Peacemaker had reached the angry great chief. In addition to his own power, Atatarho also had advisors who told him they could see the future. Those men prophesied that his way of war would be ended by two men who would come to him from the direction of the rising sun.

Atatarho had been given this prophecy even before Okwaho's family and the others had separated themselves from Onondaga. But they knew nothing about the Peacemaker when they left. Atatarho had managed to keep his people ignorant of the fact that a Peacemaker had been sent by the Creator and was coming to them.

After hearing that prophecy, Atatarho had sent spies to the east to find out who those men who would threaten his rule might be. That was how he had found out about the one now named Hiawatha. Hiawatha was, his spies told him, the first of the Peacemaker's new leaders, the one who would be by his side when he brought that Great Peace.

"NO," Atatarho had thundered. "This must not be!"

Then he made a plan. The prophecy said that two men would end his way of war. What he needed to do was to eliminate one of them. Then the prophecy could not come true. But which should he get rid of? That one called the Peacemaker seemed to have great power and it might not be possible to do anything to affect him. Hiawatha, though, did not have such power. He would be the one to strike.

Sending warriors to try to kill Hiawatha might not work. The Flint Stone People were powerful and might defend him. Doing that might also result in his Onondaga Nation finding out about the Peacemaker.

So his advisors suggested another tactic. Evil medicine could be used to destroy Hiawatha's family. That would drive him insane and defeat the prophecy by preventing him from ever coming to Onondaga.

Atatarho's evil plan seemed to work. One by one, Hiawatha's beloved daughters died. With the death of his third daughter, Hiawatha became so burdened with sorrow that he could not bear the sight of another human being. He left his village and disappeared into the forest.

Carries paused in his story, looking out over the peaceful village below.

Okwaho sat nodding his head. It all made sense. Of course Atatarho would want to end any threat to his way of war. And Okwaho did not doubt that Atatarho had the power to kill anyone who stood against him by ways other than arrows or clubs or spears. He was truly evil and frightening.

While they were still at the big village, Okwaho's mother, Wolf Woman, had cautioned him about their treacherous great chief.

"If you are ever invited into his lodge, my son," she said, "be careful what you eat or drink. Do not refuse anything, for that would be an insult to him. But only pretend to put it into your mouth. If he ever sees you as a threat, he may poison you."

Carries took a breath and let it out slowly. "Hiawatha's loss was great. But his story did not end there. The Peacemaker heard what had happened and went looking for him. I shall tell you now of how he healed Hiawatha."

The Peacemaker found Hiawatha deep in the forest, far from any village. He was sitting in a clearing by a cold campfire. It was easy to see that he had been living like a wild animal. His body was unwashed and nearly naked, his hair was dirty and matted. He had gathered snail shells from a pond and strung them on a deerskin cord. Those strings of shells were hanging from a little rack he had made of forked sticks. As he ran his fingers over those strings, he talked to himself.

He spoke to himself about how he had found those shells glittering in the shallow water of a little pond. He had picked them up one by one and begun to string them together, feeling as if each shell represented a tear he had shed for his daughters, a part of the sorrow that weighed so heavily on his mind.

"If only," Hiawatha said, "someone could lift that sorrow from my heart like lifting a string of shells from this rack." He looked at a piece of deerskin cloth he'd placed on the ground next to those strings. "If only someone would wipe away my tears."

The Peacemaker approached him quietly. No one could move more silently than he. Soon he was standing behind Hiawatha, who still had not noticed him. The Peacemaker continued to listen to the words being spoken by that lost, lonely man. "If only," Hiawatha said again, "someone could lift my grief from me the way one might lift up one of those strings of shells."

Even though he was mad with sorrow, those words Hiawatha spoke were clear. The Peacemaker recognized the wisdom of those words. It was the sort of wisdom that comes from the Creator.

The Peacemaker reached down and lifted up one of those strings of shells and that piece of deerskin. As Hiawatha looked up into his calm face, the Peacemaker began to speak.

"If anyone is as burdened by grief as you are, I will wipe away the tears from their eyes so they can see again."

Then he took that soft deerskin cloth and wiped the tears from Hiawatha's eyes.

Picking up the second string of shells, he said the second words of condolence. "From the ears of that person I will take away whatever is preventing him from hearing these words."

One by one he lifted those strings of shells and spoke

those words of condolence. The clouds of sorrow lifted from Hiawatha's shoulders, his eyes became clear and he stood up straight.

Carries reached down to his belt where his two deerskin pouches hung. He did not choose the larger one with the design of the tree on it. Instead, he untied the smaller pouch, opened it, and took out a string of shells.

"Here," he said, "hold out your hand."

Then he placed that string of shells on Okwaho's outstretched palm.

chapter fourteen
REMEMBERING

As he held the string of shells Carries had given him, Okwaho found himself remembering yet again how it had been when he and his two best friends had been together. But this time he was not remembering it with sorrow choking his throat. This time, that memory was bringing a smile to his face.

As Carries told him the story of the healing of Hiawatha, it had been as if Okwaho were there, watching it happen. Okwaho had not just seen the Peacemaker lifting the sorrow from the shoulders of Hiawatha, he had felt the sorrow being lifted from Hiawatha's mind. And he had felt more of his own anger and desire for vengeance being cleared from his mind by that story like the wind from the south blowing away the snow clouds in spring.

He handed the string of shells back to Carries.

"Niaweh," he said. "Thank you."

The tattooed man smiled and the fish twitched its tail at the edge of his lips. "Do not thank me," he said, "thank The One Who Grasps the Sky with Both Hands, the one who has sent us the Peacemaker."

"I'll do that," Okwaho said. "I'll speak my thanks and offer tobacco to the fire. But when will they come here? When will I see Hiawatha and Tsakonsaseh and the Peacemaker?"

"Soon," Carries said. "The time is not yet, but soon."

"What can I do until then? I want to help bring this peace."

Carries put the string of shells back into his pouch, tied it, and hung it on his belt.

"I was told by your mother that you like to sing?"

"That's true," Okwaho said.

"Then imagine a song of peace. Keep it in your mind and let it guide you. When the Peacemaker arrives at last at Onondaga, when he stands before Atatarho and speaks to him of peace, you will be ready to be among all those who stand behind the Peacemaker and support his message. Then the Longhouse of One Family will be established."

Okwaho nodded. He could almost hear that song in his mind already, a song as sweet as the singing of the birds or the voice of the warm wind from the summer land melting away the snow of winter.

"I have other villages to visit now," Carries said, looking down the hill. He pointed with his chin in the direction of the sunset land. "As far as the Great Hill People. They, too, will come to Onondaga when the time comes. Their villages have also been visited by the Peacemaker and they are ready to embrace peace. Those of us who've been chosen to be messengers are traveling now to remind them to begin making their way there. When the people representing all five of our nations have gathered there, then it will be time."

Okwaho felt his heart beat faster. That time would be soon! From Onondaga a good runner could reach those farthest Great Hill villages and be back within a handful of days. It would take longer for a large group of people to travel that distance, but it still meant that they could reach the Onondaga lands from their own homeland in less time that it took for Grandmother Moon to become full.

"I'll be ready," Okwaho said.

"I know you will, my young friend."

chapter fifteen
THE SONG

The song woke him. He had first begun creating it right after Carries departed. Each day he heard it more clearly in his mind. It was coming to him each morning from the chorus of birds singing to herald the arrival of a new day. It was being brought on the breath of the wind. It was in the waters of the creek as it rushed over the stones.

For two handfuls of days he had been thinking of the song. He hummed it under his breath as he walked or worked. But he did not sing it out loud for anyone else to hear. It had not yet told him it was ready.

Until now.

The song seemed to be coming from everywhere and nowhere at one and the same time. It was strong, complete, waiting to be sung.

Okwaho sat up and looked around their longhouse. For the first time in a long time, he had been untroubled by bad dreams. Nor had he remained in his sleeping rack long after everyone else.

No one else seemed to be awake. He climbed down quietly from his sleeping rack and slipped outside. The first glow of light before dawn was enough for him to see his way. He went to the hill that looked out over their village, climbed to his favorite spot, the place where Carries had spoken to him the words of condolence. He sat down and placed his back against the giant cedar that grew there.

He looked around. No one was to be seen. That was good. He was not sure he wished anyone to hear this song yet. He began tapping his palm against one of the exposed roots of the old tree, making a sound almost like the beat of a water drum. Then he began to sing.

"Aee, aee, yai," he sang. "Aee, aee, yai."

As he sang, he felt as if the song was singing itself to him.

"Aee, aee, yai," he sang.

He did it again and again, feeling more certain that this song was a good one, a song that called for what was most needed among all the people.

Then he stopped. Though he had not heard or seen anyone, he suddenly had the feeling that he was not alone. But for some reason he could not explain, he did not feel afraid about someone coming up on him unawares.

"Keep singing, little bird," a gentle voice said from behind him. It was a deep teasing voice that called him a little bird. That voice was so gentle, so pleasant to hear, so full of kindness, that Okwaho was not startled.

He turned to look. A tall man dressed in white deerskin stood there, smiling down at him. The light of the rising sun was shining on him, so brightly that it seemed as if the light was also coming from him.

"May I join you?" the man in white deerskin asked.

Okwaho nodded, finding it hard to speak. He knew who this man had to be.

He touched the ground in front of him to indicate the man should have a seat. The tall man lowered himself gracefully to sit cross-legged across from Okwaho.

"Would you continue?" the man asked. He spoke with a Wendat accent, but his words were perfectly clear.

"Keep . . . keep singing?" Okwaho said.

"Yes," the tall man said. "I like that song. Will you teach it to me?"

Okwaho found it hard to reply. This man was the one everyone had been talking about. The Peacemaker. But what could he, a boy of no importance, say to such a person? Despite what Carries had said, why would the Peacemaker come here to their little village? Was he not needed more in other places that were bigger and more important?

The Peacemaker smiled at him, as if hearing Okwaho's thoughts.

"You wonder why I am here?"

Okwaho nodded.

"I have heard of this small village of people who seek to leave the trail that leads to war. The Oneida people I just left spoke to me of this place—a place that began trying to find the path of peace even before hearing the message I am bringing from our Creator. I knew then that the people of your small village must be women and men of great courage. I knew I would need such people by my side when I go at last to meet with Atatarho."

The Peacemaker looked at Okwaho. "Are you the one named Okwaho?"

Okwaho was stunned. How could the Peacemaker know his name?

"You know," the Peacemaker continued, "before the Oneidas heard and grasped my message, they thought you people were foolish. Trying to find a path of peace in the midst of continual war. In fact, three of those Oneida warriors told me they had raided here about two moons ago. They had expected your men to respond. They were surprised when there was no reprisal, especially because they took a boy of your age captive."

Okwaho took a breath. The Peacemaker was talking about Tawis.

"The boy they took," Okwaho said. Then he stopped. Words were failing him.

"Go ahead," the Peacemaker said.

"He was my friend, my best friend."

"Ah, then you are the one who escaped them?"

Okwaho nodded.

"They were sorry they could not catch you. They were sure you would make a good Oneida. They learned your name from the boy they took. Tawis?"

Okwaho nodded again.

"You are wondering now about your friend?"

"Yes."

The Peacemaker smiled. "He is well," he said. "And making trouble for them. He tried to escape many times before they convinced him it was no use. The family that chose to adopt him are kind people. Instead of punishing him, each time he was caught and brought back, they just treated him better, calling him their beloved son, giving him the best food to eat and a comfortable place in their lodge. They gave him the name of their boy who was his same age when he drowned."

The Peacemaker's words made Okwaho both happy and sad. Happy that his friend was alive and being well treated. Sad because when someone accepted their adoption, they almost never went back to their old life. He had both found and lost his friend at the sametime.

The Peacemaker placed his hand on Okwaho's arm. "You may see your friend again soon," he said. "When all of the other nations go to Onondaga, his new family will come as well and they will have him with them."

"Thank you," Okwaho said. He took a deep breath. He had to tell the Peacemaker what had been in his heart for so long, what had been twisting his mind.

"When they took him," Okwaho said, "all I could think about was vengeance. I wanted to kill them. I was full of anger. But now . . ."

"Now?"

"Now, with what you've told me, my mind has finally become clear. It's no longer twisted with anger."

He wanted to say more, but again could not bring words forth. All of his long days and nights of worrying about Tawis would now be in the past. His friend was alive. He was well. And they would see each other again soon. It was almost too much good. He couldn't keep from smiling.

"Thank you," he managed to say.

The Peacemaker smiled. "Thank our Creator," he said. "That is where all good comes from. Kind thoughts, peace . . . and songs."

Okwaho nodded.

"So, will you share your song with me now?" the Peacemaker asked. He sat back and began tapping his hand on the cedar root next to him, finding the same rhythm Okwaho had been using.

Okwaho took a breath and began to sing. "Aeee, aee, yai." He sang softly at first, but as he continued to sing, he could feel the song itself wanting to be heard and his voice became louder.

"Aee, aee, yai."

The fourth time he sang it through, the Peacemaker joined in, his voice strengthening the song.

Okwaho had not told him it was meant to be a song for peace, yet he could feel that the Peacemaker understood that.

Words began to come to him. Words that spoke of how important it was to have peace. Peace was needed for the little children. It was needed for the elders. It was needed for all the people. Each time Okwaho sang new words, the Peacemaker sang them back to him. It was as if the song were embracing them the way a loving mother would hold her children.

He was not sure how long they sang together. But when he stopped, the Peacemaker stopped with him in perfect unison. Okwaho looked up. Elder Brother, the Sun, had risen more than the width of three hands up into the sky. It was mid-morning.

"Niaweh," the Peacemaker said. "Thank you, little bird."

He rose to his feet. "Now I must go. Tomorrow will be a busy day for all of us."

"Tomorrow?" Okwaho said.

"Yes, tomorrow is the day. All of the four nations will gather on the other side of Onondaga Lake. We are meeting Tsakonsase, the Mother of Nations, there. The Great Peace cannot be completed without the Mother of Nations bringing the power of women to us. Then our canoes will cross the lake together. We will walk as one to the place where Atatarho sits."

"How many will come?"

"Hundreds of canoes."

Okwaho drew in a breath. He could already see it in his mind. Hundreds of canoes crossing the lake together would be amazing. Even Atatarho might be awed by that!

The Peacemaker nodded. "It will be a great thing to see. And you will have a good place from which to see it. Those of your village have agreed to be waiting on this side of the lake to join us as we leave our canoes."

Okwaho could barely contain himself. He wanted to shout, to leap up and down. But somehow he managed to control himself and speak calmly the only words he could think to say.

"Niaweh! Thank you," he said. "We will be honored."

"One more thing," the Peacemaker said. "May I have

permission to carry this song of yours? I think it will be of use."

Okwaho nodded, but he also had to say something, words that came spilling out of his mouth like water from a dam that had broken.

"I cannot say that song belongs to me. It came to me. It gave itself to me. It wanted to be heard. I am not the one to give permission. It is the choice of the song itself. I believe it wanted to give itself to you. Carry it with you, please. But do not say it came from me."

A broad smile came over the Peacemaker's face. It was like seeing the sun rise above the clouds. "Shall I say then that a little bird gave this song to me?" he asked.

Okwaho smiled up at him. "Yes, that would be good."

chapter sixteen
A THOUSAND CANOES

It was a day so calm that the clouds, still glowing from the rising sun, did not move or change shape in the sky above the lake. Okwaho and all the people of their small village watched from the shore in a small cove just to the south of Atatarho's rock. They could not be seen there by Atatarho and everyone from the big village. It would be dangerous if Atatarho or any of his warriors spotted them. He might give the order to attack them and they would be wiped out before the Peacemaker's arrival.

Burnt Hair had scouted the big village the night before. He had seen all the warriors gather together. He had watched as they went by torchlight to follow their giant chief to the banks of the lake. Well before dawn, Atatarho and all his fighting men had gathered by the shore.

"I overheard," Burnt Hair had told everyone,

"Atatarho telling his people that he had used his mystical powers to foresee the arrival of a man who was pretending to be a messenger from the Creator." Then Burnt Hair had laughed. "As usual, he was lying to his people. We all know why he knew the Peacemaker was coming."

Indeed we do, Okwaho thought.

Word that the Peacemaker was coming had been brought to Atatarho by Carries. The Mohawk messenger had gone to tell the giant war chief that all the nations of the Longhouse People would be coming to him with the dawn.

Then, after seeing Atatarho, Carries had come to their small village to bring them the same news.

"Did Atatarho threaten to kill you when you spoke to him?" Burnt Hair had asked.

"Of course," Carries replied. "We met in secret at his council rock. No one was with us except for four of his bodyguards. *'Speak,'* he growled at me. *'Then after you have finished talking I will kill you.'"*

"What did you say then?" Holds the Door Open asked.

Carries smiled.

"I asked if he could wait until after the Peacemaker visited him. I promised to come back the day after that so he could kill me then if he wanted. That made one of his bodyguards laugh in spite of himself . . . although when Atatarho looked at him, that laugh ended as quickly as the travels of an ant when a bear steps on it.

"'Go,' Atatarho told me then. *'Come back after I see the liar who pretends to speak to the Creator. Come back here and lay your head on my rock so that I can smash your skull like a ripe pumpkin with my war club.'"*

His story had sent a shiver down Okwaho's back. Atatarho was so angry and so fierce. Powerful as the Peacemaker's message was, would it be accepted by the great war chief? It hardly seemed possible, even though Carries seemed so sure that all would end well.

Carries was not with them now. Before Elder Brother Sun went to rest in the west, he had gone back across the lake with the Peacemaker. There they would meet Hiawatha, Tsakonsase, and the many representatives of the four other Longhouse nations. That huge gathering of people would soon be crossing Onondaga Lake to confront the stubborn great war chief.

Or so Carries had said. But the dawn was already here and there was no sign of the Peacemaker.

Had something happened? Were they not going to come? Okwaho stared at the lake. The light from the sun was so bright reflecting off the calm waters that the far side could not be seen.

Okwaho's mother raised her hand.

"Listen," Wolf Woman said, shading her eyes as she gazed across the lake. "Listen."

Okwaho listened, as did all the others who heard what his mother said. A faint sound was coming to them across the bright water, a soft rhythmic splashing like the sound of the wings of water birds striking the surface before taking flight. Then, as it grew louder, coming closer, Okwaho recognized what it was. Canoe paddles, many canoe paddles being dipped into the water in perfect unison.

Holds the Door Open dropped to one knee next to Okwaho and put his arm over his son's shoulders. "Look, Okwaho. Look there!"

Far out, not quite at the middle of the lake, bright shapes as white as seagulls were rippling into view. Canoes, big canoes each holding several paddlers and just as many passengers. Canoes made of glistening white stone. Then, remembering one of the stories Carries had shared with them, Okwaho realized the canoes were made from the bark of white birch trees—just like the one the Peacemaker used to reach the lands of the Longhouse Nations. In the moons since his arrival, he must have shown people how to make such canoes, ones that looked to be much swifter than the heavy dugouts the Five Nations always used before.

As the great gathering of boats came closer, Okwaho

began to count the canoes. Ten, twenty, forty, a hundred. He shook his head. There were too many to count. It was as if the surface of the lake had come alive, transformed into water craft. There were hundreds of canoes approaching, covering the surface of the lake—perhaps even a thousand of them.

A thousand canoes filled with people!

Something like this had never happened before. What a great thing it was to see, all of the warriors, clan mothers, and chiefs of four of their great nations joined together for one common purpose. That purpose was to bring the Great Peace to Onondaga and unite all five of their nations.

Suddenly the idea of peace actually being accepted for his Onondaga people no longer seemed to Okwaho like a wishful dream. Even with all of his warriors, Atatarho would be far outnumbered.

chapter seventeen
COMBING ATATARHO'S HAIR

The canoes did not land where Atatarho and his war-riors were waiting on the shore. That was a good decision. Before they landed, he might have given the order to shoot arrows at them. Instead, the great flotilla came straight into the cove, with its wide shoreline, where the people of Okwaho's little village waited for them.

The Peacemaker was the first to step onto the shore, lifting himself gracefully from his canoe to stand tall. There was a gentle smile on his face. Similar smiles seemed to be on all of the relaxed happy faces of the men sharing his canoe. Those men from his canoe were clearly Flint Stone People, as were those in the many canoes surrounding his. The delegations from each of the four nations were grouped together as they landed. So many, many people. Hundreds of canoes of Swampy Land men were off to Okwaho's right. Even more Great

Stone canoes were beyond them, while farthest down the beach was the equally large Standing Stone group. They were so far away that he could not make out any of their faces, even when he squinted his eyes.

Okwaho knew which nation was which from the arrangements of eagle feathers on their caps. The Senecas had one erect eagle feather on top. The Flint Stone Nation had three erect eagle feathers. The Standing Stone People two up and one down. The Swampy Land Nation wore one lying down. While Okwaho's own Onondagas had one standing eagle feather and one eagle feather lying down.

But those Flint Nation gustowehs were different from any of the caps that Okwaho had seen the men of his Onondaga people or any other Longhouse man wear. Those fitted hats, which covered the tops of men's heads to provide them with some protection from arrows or the blows of war clubs, were usually made from thick leather or ash splints. He could see that the caps worn by the Mohawk men probably had that same construction. But there was a difference. Instead of just having eagle feathers on top, those Flint Stone Nation gustowehs were decorated with many split turkey feathers, placed all around their cap. It fascinated Okwaho so much that he turned his attention from trying to see if a certain person might be climbing out of one of those Standing Stone canoes.

"Do you see how different our gustowehs are?" a familiar voice said from behind him. It was Carries.

"I do," Okwaho said. "Why are there so many split feathers on them? They look like the turkey feathers we fasten to arrows."

"Ah," Carries said. "Your eyes are good, my young friend. That is exactly what those feathers are—split feathers from arrows."

Carries smiled broadly in that way of his, making his facial tattoos dance. Okwaho sensed that he was waiting for him to ask more, that those split feathers were part of . . .

"A story," Okwaho said. "There is a story about those feathers, is there not?"

"There is," Carries replied. "As you know, an arrow without feathers cannot fly straight. A few moons ago the men of one of our Flint Stone villages were so excited when they heard the words of the Peacemaker that they decided the first thing they needed to do was to make peace with the Standing Stone village closest to them— a village that had been at war with them for as long as anyone could remember. They rushed to that village as fast as they could.

"*'We are here to make peace with you,'* they said to the village elders when they reached the town of their former enemies.

"'If you are here to speak of peace,' the Standing Stone elders said, 'then why have you come here carrying weapons of war?'

"That was when our men realized they had made a mistake. In their excitement they had forgotten to leave their bows and arrows behind. But they knew what to do to prove their sincerity. They removed all of their arrows from their quivers and stripped the feathers from them. Then, as a further sign of their intent to truly make peace, they fastened their feathers onto their gustowehs. Like mine," Carries said, placing his hand gently on the feathered side of his cap. "It has now become the custom of all our men. And I think men of our other nations will all soon be doing the same."

"I like that story," Okwaho said. Then he looked again toward the Peacemaker. A tall Mohawk man and a woman elder with a kind, strong face had come from two other canoes to stand by the Peacemaker's side.

"Who are those people?"

"Who do you think they are?" Carries asked in a teasing voice.

"Hiawatha and Tsakonsase?"

Carries just smiled.

The Peacemaker looked over at Okwaho and Carries. He nodded his head and then turned to look at Hiawatha and Tsakonsase.

"Is it time?" he said in his soft voice, a voice that could not be heard from far away.

"It is time," Tsakonsase said.

"It is time," Hiawatha repeated.

The Peacemaker lifted his right hand, two fingers pointing upward toward the sky land. Then he dropped his palm.

Understanding his friend's signal, Hiawatha spoke. Unlike the Peacemaker's voice, his voice was so loud and clear that Okwaho did not doubt that everyone, even those farthest away along the shore, could hear him.

"IT IS TIME TO BRING THE PEACE TO ATATARHO."

"YES!" the gathered people responded with one voice, so loud that it echoed back to them from the far side of the lake.

"AS WE WALK, WE SHALL SING TOGETHER. WE SHALL SING THE SONG OF PEACE TAUGHT TO THE PEACEMAKER BY A BIRD."

Then, as Hiawatha, Tsakonsase, and the Peacemaker led them, everyone began to walk toward the place around the bend in the shore where Atatarho was waiting. And as they walked, they sang together the song that had given itself first to Okwaho and then to the Peacemaker.

AEE, AEE, YAI

AEE, AEE, YAI

It seemed to Okwaho that he could feel the song gaining power from all those hundreds and hundreds of voices joined together, voices of the people of all five of their nations. They sang to bring an end to vengeance. They sang to bring an end to grief, of mothers weeping for the loss of their children. They sang to bring an end to such loss. They sang for the innocent children and those yet to be born. They sang for those children who would grow up surrounded by love and not anger and fear. They sang for the elders who were near the end of their journeys on this earth and deserved to enjoy their last seasons in peace, surrounded by those they loved. They sang for the end of warfare, of brother killing brother. As they continued to walk and sing, the presence of peace grew stronger and stronger around them, carrying them forward.

They rounded the corner and Okwaho saw that Atatarho and his warriors were standing by his rock. None of them were moving. The presence of so many people, the sound of so many voices joined together in praise of peace, was more awe-inspiring than any weapon. The Onondaga warriors and their giant chief stood there as if they were frozen in place, unable to move as the great crowd of singing men and women and young people came closer and closer, led by Tsakonsase, Hiawatha, and the Peacemaker.

The Peacemaker raised his hand again and the people

stopped walking. He lowered his hand and although the singing ended, the powerful feeling brought by that song remained. It hovered like a great eagle with its wings spread over their heads.

To Okwaho it felt as if the air were trembling around them. What was it that had descended upon them? It was as if a great wave were washing over them. But instead of drowning in that wave, they were sharing a strength, an energy unlike anything he'd ever felt before. It was not just that they outnumbered the hostile Onotakas. This sacred power that surrounded them all was so great that no one, not even Atatarho, could resist it.

The Peacemaker and his two companions walked forward until they were almost close enough to the giant warrior chief to touch him.

"We have come," the Peacemaker said.

Atatarho opened his mouth, but no words came out.

"We have come," the Peacemaker repeated.

"Who are you?" Atatarho managed to say in a voice that was hoarse and uncertain. It sounded nothing like the roar of a great bear.

"You have heard of us," the Peacemaker said.

"Yes," Atatarho answered, his growl almost a whisper.

"We have come, all of the Five Nations brought together. We have come to form the great longhouse of one family, the longhouse of peace." He looked toward Tsakonsase. "Here is the Mother of Nations," the Peacemaker said. "Will you abuse her as you have abused all other women?"

Atatarho lowered his head. "I cannot," he said, his voice even smaller than before.

The Peacemaker looked to Hiawatha, who stood by Tsakonsase.

"Hear this," Hiawatha said. "Tsakonsase stands for the women who are the mothers of all our future generations. From this day on, she and all the women of our nations will always be respected and heard."

Hiawatha moved to the side and Tsakonsase stepped forward. She reached out to Atatarho and took both his hands.

"I now take from you all of the aggression that you have held for so long," Tsakonsase said.

Okwaho saw that Atatarho's hands were trembling as she held them. The look on the giant man's face was changing, from uncertainty to something like . . . what was it?

It's relief, Okwaho suddenly realized, remembering how much of a burden his own anger had placed on him. *Atatarho has carried his thirst for revenge for so long that being freed of its weight must be a relief.*

Hiawatha came forward. He placed his hands on the huge chief's shoulders.

"I will clear your mind from anger and violence," he

said. He reached up and began, one by one, to untie the snakes from Atatarho's matted hair, releasing them to crawl away and disappear into cracks beneath the great stone. Then, with a bone comb that he took from a pouch at his side, he combed straight the war chief's tangled locks.

"Now," the Peacemaker said, "do you accept the Great Peace?"

Atatarho was standing straighter than he had ever stood before. His eyes no longer seemed dark and troubled.

"I accept it," he said, his voice growing clearer and surer as he spoke. "I accept the Great Peace."

chapter eighteen
OF ONE FAMILY

Okwaho listened as the Peacemaker continued to speak, his words repeated by Hiawatha in that loud clear voice everyone could hear.

It was obvious that much planning and much thought had gone into what the Peacemaker said as he laid out the plans for the future of the Great Peace. He explained how there would be fifty men, each chosen by the women of their clans, to be royaners, ones who would represent their nations in council. Those councils would always be held at Onondaga, and Atatarho himself would head those council meetings where nothing would be decided until everyone agreed, until all their minds were as one.

Atatarho, the man whose name everyone had feared, would now be the strongest defender of peace. His name would be given to his successor after his own days on earth were done. A man known as Atatarho, the

Entangled One, would always head the Great League of Peace. Although he came from the Bear Clan, Atatarho's successors would not be chosen by the Bear Clan's clan mothers. Instead, all the Onondaga clan mothers would choose that man. Further, he and the other forty-nine royaners had to always be men of peace. If any royaner went to war, he would be stripped of his title.

One by one, other men were called forward from the five gathered nations to be royaners. Hiawatha was one of the first. His name, too, would always be passed down like that of Atatarho.

Okwaho's heart almost burst with pride when his own father, Holds the Door Open, was called forward— as was Burnt Hair, the uncle of Tawis.

Tawis! Okwaho suddenly thought. *Is he here somewhere?*

He began to make his way through the crowd of happy, eager people. Almost all of them were listening intently to the Peacemaker and Hiawatha, but Okwaho could see that a group of young people near the back of the representatives of the Standing Stone Nation were sitting together under a tall pine tree on a hill near the edge of the great clearing. One of them looked familiar.

As he came closer, three men stepped in front of him.

He recognized them right away. They were the Standing Stone raiders who had tried to catch him, the ones he'd called Cold Voice, Angry Voice, and Calm Voice. And behind them, sitting on that hill under the tree, playing some kind of game with four other young people, not yet noticing his friend, was none other than Tawis.

The three big men stared down at him with serious faces. They looked dangerous and threatening, even though they were not carrying weapons. Then, to his great surprise, the three of them looked at one another and smiled. Those smiles transformed them. They no longer looked like enemies. In fact, he could see something else in their faces. Kindness.

"You are a good runner," Cold Voice said, his voice warmer now,

"We have heard a lot about you from my new nephew," Angry Voice said in a friendly voice that was also a bit teasing. "Almost too much!" he chuckled.

The one Okwaho had named Calm Voice nodded and then called over his shoulder.

"My son," he called. "See who has found us."

Tawis looked up at the sound of the man's voice. Seeing Okwaho, he leaped to his feet.

"Skanoh, brother!" Tawis said, a wide grin on his face. "I greet you in peace."

Okwaho wanted to grab his friend and hug him. But this was a serious gathering. The Peacemaker and his

spokesman Hiawatha were still explaining the work-
ings of the new league. They were speaking of planting
a pine tree to symbolize the Great Peace, a tree under
whose four white roots the war club, would be buried.

He had to behave with dignity. Tawis was now holding out his arm. Okwaho reached out to grasp it, wrist
to forearm, in the old way that friends and relatives
would do when meeting each other. He wanted to say
something, anything. But his throat felt choked. His
vision was blurred. Perhaps dust had gotten in his eyes
and made them water.

But just as they were about to take each other's arms,
someone who had broken away from the crowd of
Onondaga people from the big village reached them—
at a dead run.

"Brothers!" Clouds Forming shouted as she hurled
herself forward to grab them both—with as much force
as a mountain lion leaping on a deer.

The three of them went rolling to the ground. All
of them were laughing, laughing as the people around
them were laughing. It was a good thing, this joyous
sight of friends reunited by peace. One small sign of
how the Peacemaker's dream was coming true.

author's note

There's no story more important to the People of the Longhouse, the Haudenosaunee (or Iroquois) Nations that that of the Peacemaker. At some point before the coming of European colonists, perhaps 1,000 years ago, the five original Longhouse Nations of the Mohawks, Oneidas, Onondagas, Cayugas and Senecas were engaged in what must have seemed like an endless cycle of bloody warfare with each other. No one was safe—not even women, children and elders. As my friend and teacher Chief Jake Tekaronianeken Swamp of the Mohawk Nation expressed it to me in an interview I did with him in 1992, "We were the worst people in the world."

That was when a man seen as a messenger from the Creator came to preach another way, a way of unity, peace, and equality. Because his name became so sacred that it is only spoken in ceremony, he is known simply as the Peacemaker. The result of his efforts was the formation of what has been called in English the Great League or the League of the Iroquois. Admired by such Founding Fathers as Benjamin Franklin, it has been held up as one of the models for the United States Constitution and American democracy in general.

My aim in writing this novel was twofold. First, of course, was to share with young readers a story that I feel has never been more needed in these times of conflict throughout the world. I'm trying, in a small way, to emulate Chief Swamp, who traveled all over the world during his lifetime planting symbolic trees of peace and telling the story of the Peacemaker's journey.

Second, though I have incorporated directly into the story a number of the episodes in the Peacemaker's quest, I wanted to personalize the story by seeing it through the eyes of a young person living in those times. Okwaho and the people closest to him are fictional, but the events that he hears about and experiences are deeply rooted in oral tradition.

As Tom Sakokwenionkwas Porter, another deeply respected Mohawk elder, told me on several occasions, there are so many stories about the Peacemaker that every story leads to another story. This novel came from the stories Tom and others have shared and continue to share with me and with the world—always hoping for peace.

acknowledgments

I've been fortunate enough, over the past fifty years, to hear the story of the Peacemaker directly from a great many Haudenosaunee elders. It began when I was a graduate student at Syracuse University and spending many hours on the Onondaga Reservation at the home of Alice Dewasentah Papineau, an important Onondaga Clan mother who was the first to speak with me about the Great Law of Peace. Over the following decades, aside from three years spent volunteer teaching in West Africa, I continued to meet and learn from such tradition bearers as the late Ray Tehanetorens Fadden, founder of the Six Nations Museum, Onondaga Faithkeeper Oren Lyons, the late Seneca Scholar John Mohawk, the late Onondaga Clan mother Audrey Shenandoah, and of course my friends Jake Swamp and Tom Porter. But those are only a few of the more prominent Haudenosaunee people I've known as friends and from whom I have learned.

Further, I've been able to see and interact with several new generations of Haudenosaunee women and men deeply devoted to their traditions. The story of the Peacemaker is still being told . . . and not just in words. Haudenosaunee artists are continuing to bring the story to the world through their work. In fact, a version of the story of the Peacemaker has just been illustrated by David Kanietakeron Fadden, Ray's grandson, and will be published in 2021 by Wisdom Tales Press.

I've also read all of the books written about the Great League, from Lewis Henry Morgan's classic *The League of the Haudenosaunee or Iroquois* (1851)—which was actually a collaboration with Ely Parker, who became a grand sachem of his Seneca people—on down to Mohawk scholar Brian Rice's brilliant *The Rotinonshonni: A Traditional Iroquoian History through the Eyes of Teharonhia:wako and Sawiskera* (2016), which was written after walking the route of the Peacemaker's journey, interviewing Haudenosaunee elders along the way. (I should mention that Brian spent that summer living at our Ndakinna Education Center in Greenfield Center, NY as our first Native American scholar in residence.)

Here's a very brief reading list for those who wish to find out more about the history.

Creation and Confederation: The Living History of the Iroquois (2008) by Darren Bonaparte

The League of the Iroquois (1984) by Lewis Henry Morgan

The Rotinonshonni: A Traditional Iroquoian History through the Eyes of Teharonhia:wako and Sawiskera (2016) by Brian Rice

White Roots of Peace (1990) by Paul A. W. Wallace